The passion between Colby Young and Diego Champagne grows stronger, and Diego's fear that they will be discovered grows right along with it. Violence and deception are all around them, and now with Colby as a full-fledged member of the Louisiana Banni motorcycle gang, there are new worries for Diego. He fears for Colby's safety, realizing that Colby is the most important thing in his world.

Colby continues his quest to discover what became of his young sister who disappeared years ago, and when his older sister and her children are threatened by the Texas Crushers, trouble hits close to home. He takes comfort in the arms of the man he loves, a comfort that is continually in danger of being cut off.

Meanwhile, Diego is challenged to the death by a prominent member of the Texas Crushers, and Chase, the leader of the Banni, is harboring secrets that might also result in a stand-off between Chase and Diego.

As the moonlight continues to seduce, will Diego successfully become the leader of the Banni? And if so, will a desperate Colby be able to find his place in a gang led by the man he desperately loves?

CONTENT ADVISORY: This is a re-edited, re-release title.

This book is a work of fiction. Names, characters, places, and incidents either are products of the author's imagination or are used fictitiously. Any resemblance to actual events or locales or persons, living or dead, is entirely coincidental.

Moonlight Seduction
Copyright © 2019 A.J. Llewellyn and D.J. Manly
ISBN: 978-1-4874-2505-0
Cover art by Martine Jardin

Published by eXtasy Books Inc or
Devine Destinies, an imprint of eXtasy Books Inc

Look for us online at:
www.eXtasybooks.com or www.devinedestinies.com

# Moonlight Seduction
## Rough Riders Book 2

### By

### A.J. Llewellyn and D.J. Manly

# DEDICATION

*In Loving Memory of Victoria 'Vicki' Barton*

# TRADEMARKS ACKNOWLEDGEMENT

The author acknowledges the trademarked status and trademark owners of the following wordmarks mentioned in this work of fiction:

*Autumn Leaves*: music by Joseph Kosma; lyrics by Jacques Prevért & Johnny Mercer
*Barbie*: Mattel, Inc.
*Britten / Britten V1000*: Britten Motorcycle Company Ltd.
*Café Lafitte in Exile*: Wood Enterprises
*Chase:* JPMorgan Chase Bank, N.A. National Banking Association
*The Club Ms Mae's*: 4336 Magazine St. New Orleans, LA
*Corduroy*: written by Don Freeman
*Corvette*: General Motors LLC
*Craigslist*: Craigslist, Inc.
*Designing Women*: Sony Pictures Television
*eBay*: eBay Inc.
*Electra Glide*: H-D U.S.A., LLC
*Facebook*: Facebook, Inc.
*Formica*: The Diller Corporation
*Harley-Davidson*: H-D U.S.A., LLC
*Hold On*: written by Chynna Phillips, Glen Ballard, Carnie Wilson
*Hunger Games*: written by Suzanne Collins
*Hunger Games (film series)*: Lionsgate Films
*Lone Ranger:* Classic Media, LLC
*Mary Poppins*: Disney Enterprises, Inc.
*Maury / Maury Povich Show*: NBC Universal Television Distribution
*NFL*: National Football League Association
*The Olden Days*: written by Don Mathieu

*"Life should not be a journey to the grave with the intention of arriving safely in a pretty and well-preserved body, but rather to skid in broadside, in a cloud of smoke, thoroughly used up, totally worn out, and loudly proclaiming, 'Wow! What a Ride!'"*
*— Hunter S. Thompson*

# CHAPTER ONE

Diego

Franklin fucking Kennedy. I was beginning to truly despise this son of a moron. And right now, I was just a little miffed at Colby, but it wasn't the time to get into an argument.

I was in a foul mood and ready to let it out on anyone within ten feet of me. That meant Colby because Chase was AWOL as fucking usual and I was stuck handling everything. When my phone rang, and the readout said Chase, I pulled over at the side of road on the corner of Esplanade and Burgundy to answer it.

Colby got off the bike to stretch his legs. I knew he wasn't sure where we were going or what we'd find when we got there. That probably made him anxious.

"Where in hell are you?" I said into the phone. "The last I heard, I wasn't the goddamned leader of the Banni!"

Colby's eyes widened when he realized who I was talking to.

"Calm yourself, Champagne. It's cool," Chase said on the other end. "Nuts called me. I've been in touch with Badger. Remember Kennedy's little proposition?"

"Yeah, the one about his desire to fuck me up the ass? How could I forget?"

Colby was in my face now. "What's going on? Who's fucking who up the ass?"

I put up my hand and walked away from him, trying to

concentrate on what Chase was saying.

"It's a way to solve all problems. You fight Kennedy, and they'll make a deal—even back off what's left of Death Proof."

"Are you stoned?" I snapped. "They tried to kill Colby's sister and kids. Jax is dead."

There was silence. "Nuts left that out."

"He was probably sucking on a shell, and you didn't understand him. The Texas Crushers are not about to make any deal concerning the drug trade. This is personal."

"What do you mean, personal? You broke his arm. No big deal. Is there more to it than that?"

"Long story." I glanced at Colby. One I intended to delve into a little later on.

"Badger doesn't want to take us on, Diego. They'd rather hammer out something."

"That broad Jerry was with is a virtual pot growing conglomerate. The TC want control, and the only thing standing in their way is us."

"Jax will get a proper funeral. He's a hero."

I could hear some female giggling in the background. I sighed. "If Jax is going to get a funeral, man, so is Kennedy. I'm putting him in the ground."

"That's my boy."

I gritted my teeth. I hated when he called me his boy. I wasn't anybody's boy.

"Where and when is this meeting?"

"I'm waiting for word. They want you to come with me to talk. Nuts is standing by for info."

"Good. I have Colby. Nuts and the guys can watch him."

Colby was shaking his head. He said something, but I ignored him. All I needed was for Kennedy to see Colby and go psycho on me.

"No," Chase said. "Bring him. Badger insists. He says

he'll guarantee his safety. The guys are going to keep watch over Jerry. I just talked him into signing over his share. We're now co-owners under an anonymous corporate name, Aroma Inc. Clever, don't you think?"

Jesus. Must have been some talk. Personally, I thought it far wiser to have some of our members standing by near the place we'd be meeting Badger and his merry men. You couldn't trust them. There was no reason to believe we weren't walking into a bloody ambush.

Now that we had a legal interest in the land where the goods were, there was no reason why the TC would bother killing Jerry, but then again, that Badger was one crazy mother. One never knew what he'd do.

"Diego, you still there?"

"Yeah." I glanced over at Colby, who was watching me like a hawk. "I'm here."

"I'll call you as soon I get word. They said nine-thirty. What time is it now?"

"Nine o'clock."

"Kill a half hour."

"Right."

"Look, we had a proper vote at church, voted the stragglers from the DP as Prospects. They'll be useful. We'll have a hell of a party, man."

With Chase, there was always a hell of a party somewhere—with naked women. Of course.

"Oh, and wait, Tammy wants to talk to you."

I made a face. "How many you got there with you this time?"

"Only three."

I laughed.

"Here she is."

"Hey, Tiger," Tammy said into the receiver.

"Hey, Tammy. What's up?"

"Miss you."

"That's nice."

"Chase says once all this dirty business is over with the TC, we're going to party."

"I guess."

"And I'm going to give you everything, Diego. It's been a while since you gave me some rough discipline, baby."

"I'll see you soon," I said.

She hung up after doing multiple kisses into the receiver. I put my phone away.

"You were going to leave me behind, weren't you?" Colby accused.

I straddled the bike. "I thought it best."

"Well, it wasn't best! That was my sister and kids they tried to kill, not yours."

"Well, no worries, Chase says you have to come. They want you there."

Colby eyed me. "Yeah?"

I nodded. "We have around a half hour to kill then we meet Badger and your boyfriend."

"*Boyfriend?*" Colby mouthed. "What are you talking about?"

I turned to look at him. "What could have possessed you to ball a member of the TC anyway? Were you on one of those danger trips like when you met me? How does it work anyway—the more dangerous, the more powerful the orgasm?"

"I didn't know he was a member of the TC. It wasn't like that."

"Just a stranger in a steam bath. He's fucking ugly as a hedge post."

"Bathhouses are dark. And I wasn't interested in his face." He met my gaze. "Sex is sex when you need it."

"You talk tough when you want, Colby, but mostly you're

full of shit."

"What's with you anyway?"

"You don't want to know. Anyway, I hope he was a good fuck."

Colby was pissed. I could tell by the glint in his eyes. "Well, he knew how to handle me." He lifted his head. I braced myself for more insults to come out of his mouth. "He may have been an ass, but he was better in bed than you."

I laughed.

"What's so funny? You should beef up your game if you want to compete."

*Whoa. Beef up my game eh?* I started the engine.

Colby hopped on back and folded his arms around me. "It's true," he shouted. "You may have the equipment, doesn't mean you use it as well as he does."

"Good," I hollered back, laughing. "You can tell him that when you see him tonight." I roared off into the street. I was sure if I'd turned around now, Colby's jaw would be slack.

I smiled as I drove down Esplanade Avenue, one of the quietest, most scenic, and historic major thoroughfares in New Orleans. I felt as if I'd won that one, although I still resented the fact that I was going to have to fight this guy over Colby. And even if only Kennedy and I knew it, that was the real reason.

We'd both had a taste of Colby, an especially forbidden and all-encompassing one. The victor could tell himself that he was the better contender, in and out of the bedroom. Unadulterated macho crap. But there was no backing down.

I tried to push it all from my mind and enjoy the ride. In the nineteenth-century, Esplanade was important as a portage route of trade between Bayou St John, which linked to Lake Pontchartrain and the Mississippi. Many nineteenth-century mansions still lined the street that once functioned as a 'millionaire's row' for the Louisiana Creole section of the city, similar to that of St Charles Avenue for the Anglophone section in uptown New Orleans.

Esplanade formed the boundary between the French Quarter and the Faubourg Marigny. On its very first block was the old U.S. Mint, built in the early eighteen-hundreds. The Mint produced currency for both the United States and the Confederate States over its seventy-year history and was open for tourists.

Directly opposite the Mint—branching off Esplanade—was the beginning of Frenchmen Street, a two-block-long music and entertainment district, a lively district for tourists and locals looking for a change from Bourbon Street.

As we moved away from the river and across North Rampart Street, I reached the boundary between the Treme neighborhood, made famous in the TV show of the same name, and the city's Seventh Ward. The Seventh Ward was once a multigenerational Creole enclave. Up ahead was the Esplanade Ridge/Faubourg St John section of the city, characterized by elegant two and three-story townhouses and a large number of whitewashed, black-trimmed Creole mansions surrounded by wrought-iron fences and neatly manicured lawns and gardens.

I loved this city, and I loved the distinct neighborhoods that spoke of history and diversity—my history and diversity. People would say I was nuts to feel peaceful in this city, which had a high murder rate and was saturated with violence, but when I was stressed, a drive along this route calmed my soul.

Finally, I pulled over in front of a small tavern and checked my watch. Chase would call me at any time now. But first, a drink. As always, I figured this could be my last night, and if it was, I didn't want to go out without a small glass of whiskey in my gut.

Colby touched my bicep as I stepped off the bike. "Why does Kennedy want me there?"

"Maybe he wants to reminisce with you about your encounter in the bathhouse." Yes, it was cocky. But then, I was in that frame of mind.

Colby gave me a murderous look. "You're pissing me off."

"I know." I smiled.

"And to think I was about to apologize."

"You don't owe me an apology."

"Yes, I do. I said you couldn't fuck."

"Oh?" I raised an eyebrow. "I can't fuck now. I thought you said I wasn't as good a fuck as Kennedy. Now, I can't fuck at all? Maybe you should stop while you're ahead, Colby."

He started to laugh. "Maybe I should."

"Come on. I need a drink. I might not know how to fuck, but I know how to drink." We were on the way to the door when my cell phone rang. I swore. It was Chase.

"Yeah?" I said, putting the receiver to my ear.

"Lamb Road, the industrial park . . . Old Port. The TC have a warehouse there. I'm heading there now. Can we meet up?"

"Sure. You alone?"

"They asked for the three of us. Badger says he's with Kennedy and Spike, his VP. He gave me his word. Given the nature of what Kennedy is accusing, I think it's better this way." He hung up.

I sighed. "Come on. We got to go. We got a meeting in the industrial park in the Old Port."

Colby looked hesitant. "He tried to kill my family. He's going to kill me."

"No," I said. "Believe me. He doesn't want to kill you. Listen. He's going to accuse you of coming on to him. You need to say you were very drunk. Some of the guys left you on your own. You remember nothing."

"And what about him? What's he going to say he was doing there?"

"No reason to mention where you were. He's not going to admit to being there anyway. Just save his face. Say you were drunk, and you didn't know what you were doing, and you'll walk out alive."

"He won't let it go at that."

"Oh, I know," I said. "He's got another plan, but that's my problem, not yours."

"What do you mean that's your problem?" Colby's eyes narrowed. He stood in front of my bike, blocking my path.

I smiled at him. "You'll see. I don't want to spoil the surprise."

"And why would you be implicated in all this? I'm the one who fucked him."

I pushed him aside and hopped on the bike. "He knows I've had you," I handed Colby a helmet. "And . . . he doesn't like that idea much."

"You told him about us? What were you thinking?"

"I didn't tell him shit. We had a discussion, and he assumed that I'd had you. Didn't go over well."

Colby mumbled something and put on his helmet.

We were off.

As I drove, I was thinking about the first time Colby, and I met. I was driving to the bike rally in Houston, and he was in a car. We were in traffic, and he started catcalling to me. It was crazy. I didn't know he was a member of Death Proof then, a fairly harmless small bike club that the Banni didn't really worry about. Now their leader, Jerry, had involved himself with a woman who was heavily into drug harvesting. Our biggest rivals, the Texas Crushers, didn't intend to sit by and let this huge business venture just slip through their fingers. So there was that, and the Texas Crushers attempt to wipe out what remained of Death Proof. We took the DPs under our wing for protection and got ourselves a piece of the pie, but there were a lot of personal complications that just wouldn't go away.

*Colby.* Colby was my personal problem. Big Time. He'd initiated it, whistling at me on my way to a bike rally. It took balls to do that to the sergeant in arms of the Banni motorcycle club. Then I saw Colby again at the campgrounds, where he invited me to his hotel suite. Foolishly, I went. We had mind-blowing sex, then he basically told me to hit the road, gave some speech about only having me once, then decided to have me again anyway. Go figure. No wonder I was dizzy. Colby was something else. He could rain hot and cold on me in a heartbeat. He was sexy as hell and completely uninhibited. He wanted what he wanted, and he wasn't shy about it. There was a part of me that was attracted to the unpredictable, the rush of it all. Was I going to make it to the finish line? Make that touchdown or not? It reminded me of football of course . . . my heart racing as someone tried to hold me back. When I was released, I'd run like the wind, pumping like crazy . . . my heart, my cock, and . . . yes.

Colby made me feel like that, and it was dangerous. I had to find a way to resist rushing into that windstorm, stay off the field. I couldn't have Colby, even when he was in the mood to have me. I was a biker. Gay bikers were not welcome on any level. The only time I could fuck a guy would be to humiliate him. That was okay. But there couldn't be any passion in it—or feeling.

Anyway, I was using the fact that Colby had had an encounter in a bathhouse with Kennedy of the TC a while back. If I could work up some anger over the fact that Kennedy challenged me to an extreme fight because of that, maybe I could stop daydreaming all the time about fucking

Colby.

I was a seasoned extreme fighter. I fought, and I won. These fights were underground, of course, and to the death—illegal in every sense of the word. Specially invited guests bet thousands on the outcome and never said a word about the broken, dead body they'd carry out. These fights were not for the fainthearted.

Now I was going to take on Kennedy, whose feelings were hurt. That was the worst, fighting a guy who'd believed you were banging the one they wanted to bang. Last time Kennedy and I had met, he'd guessed I'd fucked Colby, and he didn't like that much.

So he challenged me. This time the loser got sodomized in front of everyone—Kennedy's idea, of course, which meant either he wanted to subject me to the ultimate in humiliation, or he had a soft spot for me. I was pretty sure it was not the last one.

Kennedy's motives for challenging me were clear, although he would claim it was because last time we'd met, he'd tried to shoot me, and I broke his arm.

My motives were of a completely different nature. He'd gotten a member of the Banni killed, and he'd almost burned up an innocent woman and her children. Over a fuck? Unacceptable.

Chase was waiting for us at Lamb Road. He held up a hand when he saw me, and I pulled up beside him and turned off the motor.

"Section four," Chase said. "The warehouse is there. He said to look for the light and the bikes."

I nodded and pointed. "We need to turn around, take Downman Road."

The breeze coming off Lake Pontchartrain was cold tonight. I pulled up the collar of my leather jacket.

Chase looked over at Colby. "Your sister and the kidlets

are safe at the clubhouse."

"Thank you," he said.

"Now, Colby, keep quiet unless we ask you to speak," Chase said, pointing a finger at him.

I could hear Colby muttering. I hid a smile. He didn't take orders well, but as a prospect, he was going to have to learn in a hurry.

"Let's ride," Chase shouted.

I turned the bike around and followed Chase down toward the section lot. It wasn't hard to find. A huge aluminum structure, a light outside the door, and three bikes lined up in a row.

We slowed down and stopped, side-by-side. "Colby," Chase said. "Get on my bike. Diego, do the tour."

Colby got off. He gave me a questioning look. I got off as well and opened the saddlebag. I took a pistol out and tucked it into my jacket. I hopped back on and did a turn around the warehouse, looking for any sign that there may be more of them. Of course, there was nothing stopping them from arriving later, but that would mean war, and right now, I don't think they wanted to call too much attention to themselves.

I came back around to see that Chase was already talking to Spike. He kept Colby close by. Spike was a tall, lanky, middle-aged man with a scar running across his face. I'd heard that he'd once skinned a guy alive for borrowing his ride without asking. A meaner son of a bitch would be hard to find.

When I parked my bike and came walking over, Spike looked at me. "Diego," he said. He gave me a bow with his head. It was a sign of respect among the TC. It surprised me a little.

"Well, we're all here, so let's go in. Badger and Kennedy are waiting. If you're packing, think twice," he said.

I carefully pulled out my gun and walked over to the saddlebag. I placed it inside.

Spike nodded.

The door opened, and we followed Spike through the warehouse, surely used by the TC to store any number of stolen and or illegal merchandise. Aside from a few boxes of God knows what, the place looked pretty understocked.

We were led into one big, open room. It was empty except for Badger, the leader of the TC, and my friend Franklin Kennedy, who practically snarled when he saw me. Whoa. He really didn't like me.

I called out to him. "How's your arm?"

Chase shot me a look, which meant he didn't approve. I didn't give a shit. I laughed when Kennedy showed me his middle finger.

Badger, a short, stocky guy who wouldn't have been bad looking except for his overbite, came walking over to us. Kennedy and Spike didn't come with him. They stayed their distance.

No one was foolish enough to let Badger's size fool them. Badger was a mastermind criminal and a crack shot. He also was a trained boxer and a leader who tolerated no dissent. You did as ordered, or died for it.

When he stopped, he stopped in front of me, which I knew didn't go over well with Chase. "Diego," he said. "What a pleasure." His gaze went to Chase. "Smartest thing you ever did, recruiting this guy. Too bad the Banni beat the TC to the punch. Any time you want to join a real club . . ." He trailed off.

Chase's expression darkened.

"And Colby, is it?" Badger peered at him.

Colby wasted no time. "You fucking . . . son of . . . you almost killed my —"

Chase grabbed Colby's arm. "Shut up," he said. "I didn't

tell you to speak."

I glanced at Colby. Colby shook himself away from Chase and fell quiet, but he was angry.

"You got a member of my club killed," Chase said.

"That was unfortunate," he said. He looked at me again. "You should be leader. You know that, don't you? Everyone sees you as the leader."

"Listen, I didn't come here to be insulted by you," Chase snapped. "If you want us to leave, we'll leave."

"Wait a minute," Badger said. "We need to talk and set the date for the fight." He glanced at Kennedy.

I watched Kennedy as he approached, and noticed his gaze settle on Colby. That pissed me off for some reason. He looked at him as if he owned him, then smirked at me.

"It seems that you have a little faggot in your midst."

Again, Colby began to say something, and this time, I reached out for him. "Can I talk to you?" I asked between clenched teeth. I pulled him a few feet away. "What did I tell you?"

He tried to struggle free. There was no way I was letting go.

"He called me a—"

"Doesn't matter. Keep your mouth shut, or I'll knock you out cold." I met his gaze.

He pulled away, and I let him. I walked back over.

"He's got a temper." Kennedy chuckled.

"Look. Let's just get this over with," I grunted. "You want a fight. We got a lot of shit to settle. You killed Jax, and you almost killed an innocent woman and her kids. That's enough for me. Say when and where."

"Did you hear about the terms?" Kennedy grinned in my face.

"Yeah, you wanna fuck me up the ass if I lose. Who's the faggot now?" I met his gaze.

He went for me like a banshee, jumped me, which had me scrambling to stay on my feet when he began pounding. I got him around the waist and threw him off me. He landed on the floor a few feet away, embarrassed and pissed off.

Badger glanced over at Kennedy on the floor. He didn't look happy. He just shook his head. "It's not time yet."

He glanced back at Chase. "Kennedy claims he was accosted." He glanced at Colby, who I stepped in front of. "Is he a Banni now?"

"He's a prospect," Chase said. "And no faggot. I don't have faggots in my club."

I glanced at Kennedy, who was getting to his feet. He met my gaze. My communication was pretty clear. Don't fuck with me. We know something about each other that could be explosive. Watch what you say.

"You know," Kennedy cleared his throat suddenly. "I might have mixed this guy up with someone else. There was another guy, looked like him. It wasn't him."

Badger swore. "You said it was."

"I made a mistake. Let's call it . . . ah . . . even."

I smiled. "Doesn't solve the problem."

"What problem?" Kennedy eyed me.

Spike came over now, bracing for trouble.

"You attacked Colby's family and got a member of the Banni killed," I said, then looked at Badger. "How do you plan to make amends for that? This is our territory you're on."

Chase smiled over at me. He liked that. He liked it a lot. It was something he should have said, not me. But it didn't matter.

"The fight should settle it." Badger shrugged.

"Ah," Kennedy said, "there's no reason now, is there? I mean . . . sure, I made a mistake but . . . hey . . ." He looked at Badger. "Spike here can serve as our rep."

"Spike didn't cause the death of one of their members, Kennedy," Badger said. "No, we stick to the original plan. Loser gets the ultimate humiliation, but then the crowd will want satisfaction.

"To the death then," Chase announced.

"Perfect," Badger echoed. "How about this Friday night, right here?"

Chase nodded. "Perfect." He slapped me on the shoulder.

I smiled at Kennedy, who for the first time seemed nervous. "Can't wait."

Colby was muttering something in my ear. I shook my head at him.

"Now, there is another matter," Badger said. "About the crops. I think we can come to some agreement."

"We now own part of the land," Chase told him.

"Yes, we know," he said it as if he had a bad taste in his mouth. "But the land is in TC territory. That presents a problem."

Chase placed a hand on Badger's' shoulder. "I'm sure we can find a part to play for both clubs—one that will assure the operation works smoothly." Chase looked at me. "Diego, take Colby back to the club now. Stay with him. The rest of us are busy tonight. We'll talk tomorrow."

I nodded. "Come on," I said to Colby. "Let's go."

Colby stayed at my side as we walked out. I knew he was bursting with questions, but he was waiting until we were alone. The minute we were outside, he grabbed me by the arm. "What in fuck was that?"

"What in fuck was what?"

"You're fighting Kennedy in a fight to the death?"

"You don't think I can take him?" I smirked. "I may not fuck as well, but I sure as hell can fight better."

"I didn't mean . . . never mind. You're not doing it."

I laughed and walked over to the bike. "What are you, my

mother?"

"No. I'm not your mother . . . Jesus Christ, Diego, to the death and . . . sodomized as well? He doesn't want to fight you. I could tell. He's scared. Just cancel it."

I straddled the bike, held out a helmet.

Colby ignored it. "Listen to me, jackass. You don't have to do this. You don't have to prove anything."

"Don't you want him to pay for almost killing your sister and her family?"

"That's my job."

"No, it's not your job," I told him. "Listen to me. You are now considered to be part of the Banni. That means you are afforded its protection. I am the sergeant in arms in this club. That means I am an enforcer. I told you that before. This is my job."

The door opened just as Colby was about to protest again. It was Kennedy. "Get on the bike," I told him.

"Wait," Kennedy said, walking over.

He looked at Colby. "No hard feelings. I did enjoy our time together. And if you ever tire of . . ." He ran his gaze over me and made a face. "Of . . . nothing special, we could have ourselves a little party."

"You fucking . . ." Colby swung a punch and hit Kennedy square in the jaw.

I hopped off the bike and held Colby back as Kennedy rubbed his jaw. His eyes were filled with pain. He glared at me. "I'm going to fuck you up," he said softly. "Then I'm going fuck you until you can't breathe, then I'll cut off your balls. I'm going to let you bleed to death slowly, Champagne."

I laughed as I got back on the bike because I had no doubt Kennedy had fantasized about that . . . but it would remain a fantasy.

I eyed Colby. "You've had your fun, young man. Get on

the bike. Past your curfew."

Colby scowled at me but hopped on the back. His knuckles were bleeding.

I winked at Kennedy. then blew him a kiss. "Bye, darling. Enjoy your last few days. I'd get laid if I were you." I waved and roared off down the road.

I thought I heard Colby laughing as I headed back toward the clubhouse. He gripped me tight. I was driving fast, weaving in and out of traffic. Maybe he was nervous, or maybe he just wanted to hold onto me. I liked the feeling of him holding me like that, the weight of his body against mine. Shit. I wanted him, bleeding knuckles, insults to my fucking ability, and all. What in hell was I going to do? Sneak around in hotel rooms and fuck him when no one else was looking? Was I supposed to pretend I felt nothing when we were in the same room? Probably.

I pulled up in front of the clubhouse. It was dark except for the emergency light.

Colby jumped off. "I thought June was supposed to be here."

"Don't panic," I said. "They're safe."

I called Nuts.

"Yep, hello, Diego."

"Where are you? I thought you guys were bringing the woman and the kids here?"

"They're at your mom's."

"My mom's? Why?"

"We brought them to the club, your mom was working at the yard, and she didn't approve of the kids being in the clubhouse. She insisted on taking them to her house, and we're here with them, eating cabbage rolls. Man, your mama knows how to cook."

I laughed. "Okay. Stay put."

"Not going anywhere. Haven't had dessert yet."

I hung up.

"What?" Colby asked.

I unlocked the clubhouse. "They're with my mom — Nuts, Dave, and Marcel. My mom is feeding everyone."

"Oh." He walked in after me. "Why?"

"My mother doesn't approve of the Banni, but she loves the guys, treats them like her children. But she doesn't approve of our . . . activities. She didn't think this place was good for kids."

"Your mom sounds sweet." Colby smiled at me and closed the door.

"Yeah. She can be." I walked over to him. "Let me see your hand."

"It's okay," he muttered.

"No, it's not," I said. I took it in mine. "It's bleeding. Come on."

"Bathroom?" He grinned.

"Don't get any ideas." But damn it, I had the same idea. He followed me. I took out the alcohol spray. He "ouched" and "ahhed" as I sprayed each knuckle. "I can't bandage them because — "

Colby took the spray out of my hand. "Stop."

I met his gaze. My heart was pounding.

He reached up and unzipped my jacket. "I want you to fuck me," he grunted. "Fuck me, Diego."

I leaned down and pulled him into my arms, kissing him, my tongue moving with his. We separated, breathing hard. He grabbed my hand and pulled me out of the bathroom. He led me down the hallway and into one of the rooms where there was a single bed. He pushed off my jacket, pulled my T-shirt over my head, and I ceased to think.

# CHAPTER TWO

No inhibitions, no limits, and greedy, lusty demands that had me winded and soaked with sweat. Colby was that kind of lover. He gave everything and demanded even more in return.

It was agonizing pleasurable torture as he made me wait to be inside him. He begged me to fuck him, but it was on his terms. I was just his willing sex toy, and that was completely all right with me.

I was naked within minutes of him leading me to that room. Yet he stayed almost completely dressed while he touched me, licked me, and sucked me. He'd take me to the brink and leave me hanging, always with the promise of fulfillment.

He took me down on the tiny bed and pulled my head back by the hair. He opened his fly and fed me his cock while my own stayed hard and needy. He looked into my eyes and stroked my cheek. He called me beautiful, cried out, moaned, and swore, as I brought him to orgasm. Then immediately he crawled down between my thighs and casually fondled me. "Does it feel good?" he asked.

I bit my lip and nodded, but he couldn't see me. He didn't need to. He knew what he was doing to me. He licked around the head of my cock, then took it in his mouth, and I came. He laughed when he moved back up over my chest and kissed me as if he were inhaling me.

We entwined our fingers, and he kissed my hand, which I found rather odd but kinda sweet. His other hand moved over my chest and down to my belly. I was hard again. "Thought you wanted to fuck?" I asked breathlessly.

He kissed my chest, licked one of my nipples, then nodded against me. "I do. I want you." He didn't speak for a few minutes. I thought he'd gone to sleep. I lifted my head.

"Are you all right?"

"No. Not really. It's hard to . . . this is not what I wanted at all."

I looked at him. "Tell me what you want. I'll give it to you."

"Not in bed," he said. "I didn't mean in bed."

"I don't understand."

He leaned down over me. "You don't have to. It's better," he said, kissing me again, "if we don't talk."

"Okay," I said, and I rolled him over onto his back. I finished undressing him. "We won't talk." I kissed down the length of him, then lifted his legs. I stroked his cock and pushed a finger up inside of him while Colby's legs rested on my shoulders.

He was looking at me, his eyes shiny in the dark. I began to fuck him slowly with my finger, then pushed in another while I stroked his cock a little rougher.

His head went back, and he cried out, "Diego."

I took that as a sign. I lowered his legs and pushed him over onto his stomach. I grabbed him around the waist and raised him onto his knees, spreading his ass. I rimmed him as I continued to stroke him, handling his balls—just enough so that when I rolled on the condom, he was panting.

"Do you want me?" I leaned over and nibbled his shoulder.

"Yes-s-s."

I smiled and positioned my cock. I didn't go easy. He didn't want it easy. He never had. He wanted it hard and fast, and that got him off. Colby was a guy who liked to have sex with men — men who could handle him, make him submit and abandon control.

I grabbed his hips and pushed hard up inside him. He let out a gasp, then a whimper. "Oh . . . God . . ." He actually shuddered. "Yes . . . go, um, yeah, go."

I worked him hard, our bodies sliding up against each other, slippery, wet, every nerve ending alive and screaming. "You're mine," I grunted in his ear. "Say it, Colby. No matter who you fuck from now on, you'll always belong to me."

He cried out. "I'm coming!

He didn't say he belonged to me, but then I'd said that in the heat — and I do mean heat — of the moment.

I came hard and then pulled out of him, falling back on the bed. He moved over to where I lay and put his head on my chest. Unusual for him. I stroked his hair. He moved his hand down to my cock and ripped off the rubber and wrapped his fist around my shaft. I chuckled. "You want it again?"

He glanced up at me and nodded. "Don't worry. I'll do the prep."

I laughed as he moved back down to my cock. It didn't take long. He stroked it straight up and asked me for a condom. I found one on the nightstand. The place was condom city, what with all the biker chicks.

I watched him roll it on my cock. "Um, feels good."

"Gonna feel even better in a minute," he told me. "I'm going to ride it just like we ride those bikes out there. Only riding your cock is so much . . ." He began to guide my cock up inside of him, and I groaned. "So much more . . . Oh, Jesus, Diego, your cock is so big. Nobody has ever made me feel so . . . ooh . . . full. God damn beautiful," he hissed, bearing all the way down. I lifted my hips, and he wiggled a little. "Um. You're in . . . so in. Diego, I'm going to fuck your cock."

He did. He fucked my cock all right. I watched him, his head back as he moved up and down on me, his fingers rubbing and teasing his own nipples, and I held on as long as I could, just to watch him. Porno had nothing on Colby. When he came, he held his cock, the come sprayed my stomach, and he moved up over me and trailed it across my lips, then kissed me deep and hard.

We lay there side-by-side after that. He didn't touch me. He seemed deep in thought. I knew we had to move, get dressed. It was almost morning. We'd been fucking most of the night, and the sun would come up soon.

Colby turned to me, his head on the pillow beside me. "Can you take Kennedy?"

"Yes."

"You mean it?"

"I mean it."

"I've never seen an extreme fight. I know someone dies at the end. Are there weapons?"

"No guns, but apart from that, there are no rules."

He turned away. "Jesus Christ."

I didn't know what to say. "Why this sudden concern for my welfare?" I guess I wanted to hear the words. He didn't have to say he loved me. He probably didn't. "Colby. It's okay to care, doesn't mean we're . . . you know. No strings."

"Fuck you, Diego," he said. He started to get out of bed.

I put a hand on his arm. "Wait. You're angry at me."

He turned around and for a moment didn't say anything. He just looked at me. Then he sprang on me, lying on me. He pinned my arms to the mattress and captured my mouth. He kissed me passionately, then moved down the length of me, licking me and suckling me. He stroked and sucked my cock and my balls, and I was erect again.

"Damn you, Colby," I muttered. I made a grab for him,

22

and we rolled off the bed onto the floor. I took him there on all fours, holding him prisoner in my arms while he pretended to struggle. But we both knew what he wanted. I tightened my hold and fucked him hard while he cried out. Finally, Colby said my name while I rubbed his cock and his nipples and rode him even harder on the carpet.

We came on our knees, his back against my chest and I held him in my arms until his breathing returned to normal. He rubbed his head under my chin, then turned and held me, his lips touching my shoulder. He kissed my ear and then whispered, "I hate you for this."

I released him. His words shocked the hell out of me. I stared at him, speechless.

He reached up to touch my face, but I pushed his hand away. "Don't."

"You don't understand," he said. His eyes were bright with tears. "If I love you, I'll lose you. I lost my mother and my sister. I loved them too much. Kennedy will take you from me, and that will be it." He got up and looked down at me. He took my chin and lifted my face. "But if I don't love you, you'll be okay. I can have you when I want."

I shook my head and stood up. "No. You can't, Colby," I said. "When your membership in this club is final, it will be the end of us like this. We have to stop." It broke my heart, but it had to be said. "I can't be your lover."

The bright tears in his eyes rolled down his cheek, but he said nothing.

"Get dressed," I told him. "I'll take you to see your sister." I walked out of the room and down the hall. I stepped into the shower. My heart was heavy, but I'd keep it inside. I knew Colby didn't hate me. It just shocked me. His reasons for trying to bury what he felt had to do with his family, but the truth was, we couldn't be together anyway.

I was Banni. I would be Banni for the rest of my days. I

was indebted to Chase. It was my sacrifice, and I had no choice but to accept it. If Colby committed to the Banni, it would be the same for him. And given his past membership in Death Proof, his best chance of survival was to join our club.

The TC would always be suspicious of any unaffiliated former DP club member. It's just the way things were. I knew I had to find a way to be friends with Colby without wanting him in my bed. I didn't know how but I knew I had no choice if I wanted to keep both of us alive.

As I let the water run over me, I wasn't sure Colby understood that. Death Proof was a club without a lot of rules, and a high level of tolerance. The Banni had no such tolerance.

I stepped out of the shower, towel around my waist, and Colby opened the door. He didn't look at me for some reason. He kept his gaze on the floor. "Diego?"

"Yeah?" I took out a disposable razor.

"I know that was the last time."

I glanced at him through the steamy mirror.

"I know I could get you killed. And now that I'm joining the club . . . How do you . . ."

I wiped the steam off the mirror and scraped the razor over my jaw. "I just go off on my own and find someone, sometimes a gay bar, or—" The words stuck in my throat. I didn't want to tell Colby how to find release in the arms of another man, but I guess I needed to.

"Prostitute."

"Sometimes. You need to leave your colors behind, make sure no one knows you there."

I saw him nod.

He cleared his throat. "Thanks."

"Please, don't," I said.

He reached over and touched my shoulder. "I don't hate you."

"I know that."

"And—"

I shook my head at him.

He nodded. "Okay." He watched me for a minute. "Don't shave off the shadow. It's really sexy and . . ." He stopped. "There's only one place." He reached out and took the razor. He tipped back my head and ran the razor over one patch on my jaw. He rinsed the razor in the sink and did it again, running his fingers down my throat softly as he did. He was standing so close to me, I could feel his breath and then his soft kisses as he pressed his lips over and over in a row down the length of my throat.

"Colby," I moaned. "Stop."

His kisses intensified as his hand caressed my chest and my arm. I lowered my head, and he kissed my mouth so tenderly, his fingers moving up into my damp hair as he softly moaned.

His free hand pulled at the towel, and he dropped to his knees. "One last time, baby," he said softly, "Please, just one last time."

He didn't wait for my consent.

One hour later, we were at my mother's house. Carl, one of our guys, sat outside on the porch. I knew he was packing. "Hey, Diego," he said. "All's quiet."

"Great. Where are the others?"

"Nuts, Dave, and Marcel are all sleeping in the basement, stretched out on mattresses. It's my watch now."

"Perfect."

I walked in the door, Colby behind me. I could smell bacon cooking in the kitchen. It was almost ten o'clock.

I didn't have time to introduce Colby to my mother because when brother and sister first saw each other, they ran into each other's arms and embraced. Colby's niece and nephew also came into the circle for hugs, calling out, "It's Uncle Colby, Mama," and Colby picked them up, one in each arm, and kissed them.

I walked into the kitchen and gave them some privacy.

My mother glanced at me, poured a cup of coffee, and came over to sit it in front of me at the table. Then she went on cooking bacon. It looked as if there was a mountain of it.

"Thanks," I told her, pulling out a chair. "You cooking for the troops or what?"

"Just about. I assume that was Colby you came in with?"

I nodded, sipping the coffee. "I'll introduce you later."

"No problem. I fully understand. They're close. Need some time to reconnect. Terrible thing what happened."

"Thanks for bringing them here. This is a much better place for the kids. Hope the guys haven't been bothersome."

"Marcel beat me twice at poker last night. If you call that bothersome." She smirked. "Nuts, however, can't play poker worth a damn, gets pissed when he loses. And that boy and his nuts . . . I went crazy this morning sweeping all those shells up. Is there any way to break him of that damn habit?"

"We could put him in some sort of rehab. No nuts for a month."

"Ha, ha."

"Mom. You don't have to sweep up. Nuts will do it himself."

"Never mind. Not gonna have you boys cleaning the house now. She put down the utensil and turned off the stove. "Who in the world tried to burn down that poor girl's shop, anyway? Two little kids and all. Better not have been you fellows!" She pointed at me. "What are you into now?"

"The Banni would never condone that, Mom. You know that. It was TC, a payback thing."

"This is not TC territory. Let them buggers stay in Texas where they belong."

I smiled and sipped the coffee. "They have a chapter here."

She walked over and looked at me, stroked my hair for a moment. "You look like you haven't slept, kiddo."

I nodded. "Business." I cleared my throat and looked away.

"Sleep's important, Diego. By the way, Tammy is minding the yard this morning. I sent her over there. I couldn't leave here, what with everything. You can take it off my pay."

"I'm not going to dock your pay," I told her, laughing.

"That's okay. We'll pay Tammy."

"So, what's with you and that skinny little thing anyway? She told me there's something special with you two. I think she's hoping for a ring one of these days."

My eyes bugged out.

"Excuse me." It was Colby. He walked into the kitchen and smiled at my mother. "I want to thank you, Mrs. Champagne, for keeping my family here."

"Not a problem. And the name is Cherise. You're the brother, then."

"Yes, sorry I didn't say hello when I came in but—"

"Not a problem. I fully understand."

"So . . ." Colby gave me a look. "Who's Tammy?"

I drank the rest of my coffee. "Just a girl." I shrugged.

"Not just a girl," my mother interjected. "Tammy is mad for Diego, but he's too blind to see it. I was hoping he'd get a brain and settle down."

Colby looked at the floor. This was uncomfortable.

"Thanks." I made a face at my mother. "I think you just called your son brainless."

Colby laughed.

"Anyway, she pines for Diego and waits around. If I was that girl, I'd give this boy of mine one good kick in the ass.

Have some bacon," she said to Colby. "Excuse me. I'm going to go give a shout to those boys for breakfast."

"Coffee is made," I told Colby after my mother had left the room. "Help yourself."

He went to pour some into a mug sitting on the counter. "So, you, ah . . . go out with this Tammy?"

"No. She works for us at the scrapyard. Her uncle is a member of our club. She's been around the Banni for a while. She likes the club."

"It sounds as if she likes you in particular." Colby sipped his coffee and eyed me.

I stood. "Doesn't matter."

"Is she your cover?" he asked me, moving closer. His voice was low and sounded pained. "You fuck her every once in a while, give the poor girl some relief?"

"Sometimes."

"It's okay. I mean, they'd think it funny if you never fucked women, I guess."

"Sounds fucking logical, doesn't it?" I said between clenched teeth, then walked out of the kitchen. I didn't want to discuss Tammy with Colby.

As I came out, I almost walked right into Colby's sister. "I'm sorry." I smiled. "You must be June." I held out my hand.

"Yes," she said, shaking it. "Hello."

"Diego Champagne."

"My goodness, you're so . . . tall," she said, smiling.

I laughed. June looked remarkably like Colby. So pretty.

"Cherise is your mother," she said.

"Yes, she is."

"She's so nice."

I smiled.

Colby came out with his coffee. "Where are the kids?"

"In the other room, playing with their toys." She looked

from me to Colby. She looked at us so intently that I began to feel a little self-conscious.

"I, ah . . . need to get to the scrapyard," I said. "I'll just make sure the guys are awake and then be off."

"Tammy might need you," Colby said. "For something," he added.

It sounded innocent to June, but not to me. I didn't say anything. I just looked at him for a second, then went down into the basement to make sure the guys were getting up.

My mother was already on it. The three of them were all awake, and Nuts was even getting the vacuum cleaner out. "I'm sorry, Cherise." He looked like a naughty little boy as he went around picking up shells off the carpet.

"Well, you should be," she muttered. "I told you, you don't have to do that."

Marcel hugged her. "Do I smell bacon, Mom?"

"Get off me, you." She gave him a shove.

Marcel laughed.

"Hurry up if you want to eat. It's ready."

My mother padded back upstairs.

"Look," I told them, "I'm going to the scrapyard. You guys stay here. I think it should be fine now, given the upcoming fight, but we won't take any chances yet."

"No worries, Diego," Marcel said.

"You're taking on the TC tomorrow night," Dave said.

I grinned. "Not all of them at once."

Everyone laughed.

"You could," Nuts said with a chuckle. "All a bunch of wimps. And that Kennedy . . . I hear he's a fag. Everyone knows those limp wristed faggots can't compete with a real man. Diego will squash that little queen like a bug."

I sucked in some breath but didn't comment as the others all added their own comments. I'd heard that kind of shit over and over. I was pretty much immune.

29

"My money's on you, man," Marcel said.

"Good choice. See you later."

I went upstairs, pausing to see Colby in deep discussion with his sister and then I slipped outside. As I was getting on my bike, the front door opened. "Hey, you," my mother called out from the porch.

I looked up.

"You too good to say goodbye to your ma anymore or what?"

I got off the bike and came up onto the porch. "Sorry." I leaned down and gave her a hug.

Then I turned to go.

She hung on to my jacket.

I glanced at her. "What?"

"Tell me it's not true."

Damn it. Those guys had big mouths. They had to go and tell her about the fight. "It's not true." I grinned like I had countless times as a boy when I was caught doing something I shouldn't have been doing.

She slapped my arm. "You lie."

"It will be all right, Mama," I told her, then leaned down and kissed her cheek. "Don't worry."

"Don't worry? I worry every time you get on that bike. My heart goes to my throat, and I know one time it will be the last time I see you, Diego."

"Don't talk like that."

"My beautiful baby boy lying dead somewhere. Why do you do this? Why, Diego? You don't need the money anymore. Now, this time, this fight to the death . . . it's for what? Is it for honor?"

"I have to go," I said. I had no answer, at least not one she was going to accept.

"If you get killed," she hollered after me, "I'll never forgive you."

I waved and took off, a smile on my face. Just like my mother to say something like that.

I didn't go to the scrapyard right away. I went for a long ride on my bike, laughing every once in a while as I remembered the things my mother used to say to me as a kid. She was always threatening to 'whup' me, but by the age of ten, I was bigger than she was. Her bark was bigger than her bite, but her words had some logic to them. It was true I could easily wind up dead. My time would come, but not this time.

Tomorrow night was the fight, and I needed to get my head on straight. It was as much psychological as it was physical, and if I wasn't in the right headspace, I could very well end up dead — or worse. I'd end up with Kennedy poking me in the ass with his pathetic little prick. Nope. That definitely was incentive enough to win this one.

But I needed to be on my own until the time came. It was my ritual. I rented a really nice hotel room on Bourbon Street and called Chase on my cell phone.

"I know the routine," Chase said. "No worries. We'll see you tomorrow night. Get your head on, man. Get laid, whatever. But you gotta win this. There's a lot riding on this one."

Not to mention my hide. That was low priority, as far as Chase was concerned.

All I wanted to do was sleep. I got a bottle of whiskey, stripped off all my clothes, and drank myself into a stupor. Finally, I crawled into bed, and there I stayed until three o'clock Friday afternoon.

But rather than rest my mind, my sleep had been filled with dreams. Rather than waking up feeling peaceful and calm, like I usually did before a fight like this, I woke up swearing.

I'd dreamed of Colby. I'd dreamed of fucking him. He just kept coming back for more and I tried to hide everywhere.

But he'd find me, and every time he found me, the dreams got hotter and hotter—and more erotic.

I struggled out of the bed and climbed into the shower. I let the hot water transform me into to a living being again. I wasn't sure what kind of shape I'd be in tomorrow—most likely bruised, battered, and hurting like hell. I never once thought I'd be dead. To even consider that would be to unbalance me, weaken my abilities. I always used the old tricks my football coach taught me when I was fighting. You must keep your mind on the *now*. You have to be loose, relaxed, and let him to come to you. You block out everything—the crowd, the noise, and you concentrate only on winning. It was mental strategy, never allowing yourself to get intimidated by your opponent, no matter his size or his strength. If you make a mistake that doesn't cost you too much, forgive it, forget it, and concentrate on the next move.

I couldn't think, hey, I could be dead at the end of the night. That was as good as digging my own grave. In fact, you can't think and fight. You must go on instinct and always with the will to survive.

I got out of the shower and got dressed. I checked my phone. Chase had called twice. He left a message the last time. "Don't be late, Champ," was all he said.

There were three calls from Colby. No message. I wasn't sure what that was about. I hoped he wouldn't be there tonight.

I called Chase. "I'm on my way."

He was already there. I could hear the crowd in the background. They sounded like the Romans at the Coliseum just before some poor fuck got eaten alive by a lion.

"Good," he shouted into the phone. "We'll have one hell of a party at the end of the night. Say goodbye to Jax."

"Okay. Eh, are the new guys there, too?" I held my breath.

"About that. We had church. I thought we should get the former DP members voted in. Everyone voted yes, no problem. I knew your vote was yes so . . . didn't want to call you out of your monk retreat for the vote."

"Okay. So the entire club is there, I suppose?"

"Everyone. And shit, I never saw so many TC members. A gang of them all rode up from Austin. They got some hot chicks, man. Some of 'em look like models."

That meant Colby was there. Damn.

"I'm surprised Cledus showed up. He told me he's into this kind of thing. Likes to gamble. Bet a shitload on you."

"How is Colby getting on with his father?"

"They're talking. It seems okay."

"Great," I muttered.

"You know we love you."

"Yeah," I said. "I know. I'm on my way."

I sank down on the bed and put my head in my hands. I didn't know why I would have preferred it if Colby had stayed away. I guess I worried he'd shake my concentration. But no, I wouldn't let him. I'd fight on and . . . I swallowed. I wasn't sure how I was going to do this. Not the fight. The fight was . . . well . . . what it was, but Colby? How in the hell was I going to deal with him being in the Banni and wanting him the way I did?

I had to use the same techniques I employed to face any opponent. I had to see my feelings for Colby as something to be conquered, to be wiped out. If I didn't, we'd both end up dead. Was our love worth our lives? Jesus, we weren't Romeo and Julius!

I'd made a decision. After I won this fight, if I could still stand, I was going out by myself and get laid somewhere, with someone who could wipe out the memory of Colby's touch on my body. The passion I had for him seared my insides, and it had to stop.

I drove without my helmet tonight, letting the breeze blow through my hair. I even closed my eyes a few times on a long stretch. It felt so good. I felt free. It didn't matter what happened around the corner. I had to live in the now and riding down the road on my bike was just what I needed at the moment.

When I drove up in front of the warehouse, there were several members of the TC standing outside, smoking, shooting the shit. They got really quiet when they saw me.

I hopped off my bike, then pulled my hair back and tied it. They nodded at me as I walked by, and I nodded back. I navigated the narrow hallway to the larger room, led by the noise of the crowd.

When I walked in, there was applause, some whistles, and cheers. It was like I was a rock star. The Banni gathered round me like a shroud, patting me on the back, giving me words of encouragement I hardly heard.

My gaze was on Colby, standing a few feet away at his father's side. He was wearing a Banni patch. I swallowed.

Colby met my gaze, his expression hard to read. It could have been terror I saw in his eyes. Whatever it was, I tore my gaze away from him and vowed not to look his direction again. I couldn't. If I gave Colby one minute of thought during this, it would distract me. Since Kennedy had a disadvantage in size, he'd look for every way to distract or intimidate me, shake my confidence, and I'd be a dead man.

The guys moved off, but Chase and Nuts stood at my side. There were a lot of men here, at least two-hundred. Someone was going to lose a shitload of money, while others would be celebrating.

I stretched a little, took a few breaths. I saw Badger come out into the middle of the floor. He looked over at me. "I see you didn't chicken out, Diego," he called to me.

The members of the Banni booed loudly. I just laughed.

"Where's your boy, Badger?" Chase challenged.

"He's preparing himself."

"Preparing to lose," Chase scoffed.

The crowd reacted predictably—the Banni laughing, the TC booing, and hissing. I needed to start pretending they didn't exist. "Don't talk to me anymore," I told Chase. I looked at Nuts. "Get away and give me some space."

They both moved off, and I stood there alone, serene inside myself. The crowd was endless faces and colors blending together. The voices were barely audible, just sounds, rising and falling with an uneven bizarre rhythm.

I had no weapons. We weren't allowed guns. That would have been too easy. But a knife, a shank, a chair—anything was permitted. Often weapons got thrown in the middle of the floor during the fight because the spectators wanted a little more blood. I preferred to start without anything.

I saw Kennedy now. He stood a few feet away.

Chase and Badger came into the middle of the floor, and I moved into the center to meet my opponent. I was completely focused on Kennedy, nothing else. I was going to win, even if I couldn't control what would happen on the way to that victory.

We weren't asked to shake hands.

Badger did the introductions. I hoped to hell it wasn't going to be a long speech. "Gentlemen, if there are actually any gentlemen here, which I doubt . . . should I say instead, welcome members of the Texas Crushers, the Banni, and their special guests. And an extra special welcome to the ladies."

Kennedy met my gaze with defiance.

"Tonight, to the death with a special treat before the final breath, the winner will give the loser a special jab he won't forget before he sends him off to his great reward!"

Deafening cheers. It was really strange what people got off on.

"For the Banni, we have our sergeant in arms, Diego Champagne," Chase shouted.

Badger proceeded to introduce Kennedy, who came closer and said in my ear, "I can't wait to get a crack at that tight ass of yours."

I didn't flinch.

He backed away.

"Take off your colors and your shirts, contenders!" Badger shouted.

I shrugged out of my vest and pulled the T-shirt over my head. Marcel rushed forward and took them from me.

I heard Chase and Badger declare that the fight had commenced and then Kennedy made a rush for me. Chase and Badger jumped out of the way and raced off the floor toward the crowd.

He'd taken me by surprise, landing on me with all his weight. I threw him off me, landing a hard punch to his solar plexus, and sprang to my feet. I was ready this time. I noted the pain on his face, and when he came for me again, I grabbed him by the throat with one hand and put him on his knees with the other. I slammed him again in the same place, and I kept hammering.

Something shiny slid across the floor. I squeezed hard around his throat as he struggled for air, then I felt a blade slash across my calf.

I released his throat, looking down to see that he'd sliced through my jeans and the material was quickly getting soaked through with my blood. "You son of . . ." I muttered and grabbed for his hand. He had the knife ready to strike and, as I struggled with it, he kicked out with his boot and hit me in the leg again.

I looked down to see the knife edge sticking out of the toe of his boot. I was in pain, but I needed to manage it. He was hurting, too. I kicked out and got him right between the legs.

Nothing hurts like that. He went down and scrambled across the floor. I saw the knife fall and I kicked it away from him. I was on him, hitting him over and over. He hit me back, once in the jaw, then another hard in the chest.

I laughed at him. That made him mad. He swore at me and went for my throat. We rolled on the floor again. I got Kennedy around the neck again and he kneed me in the groin. The pain caused me to back away for a minute. I heard a sound and Kennedy had scrambled to the other side.

I saw the metal bar coming at me and I moved fast, but not fast enough. He hit me across the head, and I saw stars. For a second, I thought I was going to pass out, but the blood in my eyes forced me to stay alert.

I reared up and grabbed the metal bar, slippery with my blood. Kennedy clung to it. I pulled so hard, he almost flew across the room. He was on his back. Perhaps he'd broken it. I didn't know. I heard the sickening crunch of bone. I pulled him off the floor and, like a boxer, I hit him several times to the stomach, one uppercut, and a hard kick again landed him across the room. I couldn't stop. I was limping, wiping blood out of my eyes but there was no way I was letting Kennedy get anywhere near me with his prick. I hit him again, several times. He was bleeding heavily. I knew he was finished.

I reached down and hit him one more time, hard. He cried out, "Son of a bitch!" Then he went limp.

I couldn't see his face, in part because I could hardly see myself, and in part 'cause his face was a mess. He was bleeding like crazy.

I was losing blood, too. I felt like I'd been too many times on a circus ride. I had to finish this. He was huddled in a ball on the floor, and I picked up the pipe.

The crowd was calling for blood, and I could hardly stand up.

I felt a hand on my shoulder, and I turned to see Chase. "Your reward. Do it. Fuck the little bastard."

I went to one knee, shook my head. "No thanks!"

"If you don't, I will," Chase growled.

"No," I said, "you won't. This was not my condition; it was his. Leave it alone, Chase."

The crowd was turning around and around me. I let the sound come back. I could hear the Banni, clapping and taunting the Texas Crushers, who'd grown stone quiet, waiting. There was going to be shit in the future. I could feel it.

A couple of the Banni pulled Kennedy out in the middle of the floor beside me and yanked down his pants. "For Diego!" Chase called out. "The winner!"

Again there was screaming.

Kennedy was dying, which meant I wouldn't have to kill him. And all the while, he was going to get humiliated in the middle of the floor.

I struggled to my feet. I was going to catch hell for this later with Chase, but so be it. I lowered my head beside Chase's ear and said, "I said no. Put a stop to this or I will, and you don't want that."

Chase glared at me. No, he wouldn't want me to defy him publicly. It had to look as if it was coming from him.

Chase put up a hand. "We want to show you good faith," he called out. "We have decided to let Kennedy die with dignity. We won't claim our reward."

I glanced up at the crowd. Members of my club were complaining. Wasn't it enough the guy was dying? Did he have to die like that? No, he deserved some dignity. I'd deal with the fallout later.

I went back to my knees, reached over, and pulled the guy's pants up over his butt. He was still alive.

Chase motioned to the other guys. "Diego, take your kill."

Kennedy eyes were glassing over. He mouthed "*thank*

*you."* And then he was gone.

I felt for a pulse. I looked up at Chase and shook my head.

Suddenly, I was being lifted on the shoulders of the Banni and paraded around, while the members of the Crushers began to quietly file out of the room.

# CHAPTER THREE

Colby

The look in Franklin's eyes as the life left his body is something that will haunt me the rest of my days. It pained me, not because I still had feelings for the guy, but because he hated himself so much at the end that he was grateful to die. He looked like a twisted, grotesque mannequin lying on the floor.

It was a gruesome way to go, and I felt ashamed to have witnessed the whole thing. I knew what he'd done had caused his own demise. The man had put out a contract on me because I no longer wanted to be with him. That was at the heart of all of this.

I couldn't lose sight of that.

For one moment, we all fell silent. Then we shook ourselves into action.

Diego seemed relieved that he hadn't had to take the man's life. Franklin's lifeless body remained where it was, as some of the guys made calls, some moved around, trying to straighten up. I was in a state of shock when my father, Cledus, and his right-hand man and often abused lover, Calvin, came up to us. Cledus had doctored more crime scenes in his time than I'd had hot dinners.

"Chase, you make yourself scarce for a coupla days. Go someplace and spend some time with some real friendly women who can vouch for you."

"I ain't ashamed of what I did," Chase ground out. He

kept stroking his straggly ginger-colored beard. He kept his long hair in a braid. I always yearned to grab it from his head. I had no idea why. I just disliked the guy.

*You don't like how close he is to Diego,* a mean little voice whispered inside my head. *Shut the fuck up,* I told it back.

"No. But Teresa called the cops," my father retorted. "Unless you want a bounty on your head like my boy, Colby, I suggest you split."

"Why would you wanna take the blame?" Diego asked. He was kneeling, pressing a bloody towel to his injured leg. He stared up at my old man.

Cledus shrugged. "Makes me feel young again." He gave Diego and the others a smile that reminded me of a tomahawk. When nobody responded, he said, "My way of thanking you for taking me and my boy into your club."

He liked being the center of my attention, my old man— especially when a dead body was involved. Next, he'd be taking credit for the beating. I could just see him spitting on the ground and saying, "It was me, officer. It was self-defense, and look at all the witnesses."

"And send us a postcard," Calvin said.

*Oh, brother.*

Chase split at the first sound of a siren in the distance. I heard him start up his bike and disappear into the night.

My pa spit on the floor. Man, he needed a new routine. "Teresa squealed because she was sure Franklin would win, not the other way around," he told us.

Some of the guys present seemed surprised.

I wasn't. "Of course she did," I couldn't resist saying. "She figured she'd report a homicide, get Kennedy locked up, and keep all the profits from the grow for herself."

Cledus nodded. "Yeah. She's some kind of black widow. Seems all nice and hot to trot, but she bites. Bad. I can't stand me an uppity woman. Now, git cleanin', everbody."

The others groaned, but Cledus began bossing everybody around. I listened, only half interested in the banter. *Everybody*. When it suited him, Cledus wheeled out his country schtick, sounding like an aged, demented Jed Clampett. Sometimes I just wished he'd shut the fuck up.

"Stick to the story. Self-defense. We'll tell the cops all about Teresa's nice little marijuana operation. By the time I'm through with that bitch, she'll regret the day she fucked with my family." His evil smile, for once, gave me hope. He and Calvin took care of Franklin, calling in favors left and right on their cell phones.

Diego shook his head and gave Cledus a look. "You keep your mouth shut about the dope. We own half that property and are in negotiations with the TC."

Cledus sighed. "Okay, whatever."

Diego didn't look very happy about what was going on. I could see the tension in his face.

As the police sirens grew closer, the room thinned out. Those remaining, including a couple of the TCs, backed up the story that Diego and Franklin had fought, but it had been Franklin who started things.

"I threw the fatal blow, officers," Cledus said. But anythin' that happened to Franklin was out of self-defense."

Diego looked incredulous, but a few of the guys began agreeing vehemently. Bunch of pussies.

My mind reeled back to the time I secretly watched Cledus paralyze a man who owed him money. He had no reason to cop to this crime, except I had a funny feeling that he wanted the word spread far and wide that Cledus Young was still a man to be respected—and feared.

I tried to block the image of poor Tony trying to escape Cledus's fearsome wrath all those years ago. He's still out there somewhere, his life in tatters, as far as I know.

It didn't seem to me like the cops were ready to weep

over Franklin being dead. For a moment, I remembered what he'd been like when we'd dated briefly. His passion had been tattoo art.

If only he hadn't turned out to be a complete homicidal wacko.

We all have many facets to our personalities. I'd been charmed by the part of him that rhapsodized over the work of a legendary, long-dead tattooist I'd never heard of called Sailor Jerry. He was a man who'd spent his life in the tropics immortalizing men's fantasies of wanton hula girls.

Franklin had huge picture books of some of Sailor Jerry's most popular images. He tried more than once to talk me into letting him give me a tattoo of an anchor entwined with thorny roses.

"No roses for a sailor's grave," he'd said.

But Franklin would get a grave. And I'd make sure he'd have some roses. Well, maybe one. He couldn't threaten me, or my kin, anymore.

And I hoped wherever he wound up on the other side of this life that Franklin found peace. I wished him that—and maybe a glass or two of Kentucky bourbon with Sailor Jerry.

I was surprised when I noticed Detective Rogan Duchesne threading his way toward me.

"What are you doing here?" I asked, then remembered he worked homicide.

"Came here to post his photos on Facebook," he said sarcastically. "Maybe sell a few on eBay."

I grimaced. "I deserved that."

"Naw. I'm just in a bad mood. I was watching *Sons of Anarchy* on TV and got notification of this bullshit. You talked to June Gold about our case yet?"

I shook my head. "Haven't had a chance."

He gave me a searching look. "I think I finally understand what it is you feel about your chopper. I got me one now."

He gestured outside. That surprised me. I looked out the window. He'd bought himself an Electra Glide standard Harley.

Maybe the man had some style after all. "Look at you! What made you buy it?"

"Don't say anything, because I'm not supposed to accept things like that, but your old man got it for me." He must have noticed my shocked expression because he said, "He told me it was a thank you gift."

Another huge surprise. Thank you for what? What's with him and all these thank-yous all of a sudden?

"Talk to your sister," he said, his voice low. "I need a break on this case, Colby." He walked off, and I took a deep breath. My pa was one giant conundrum. He'd been a lousy, stinking father to me, but both of us couldn't get past the fact that my sister, Garnet Beauty, had disappeared at the age of six. My mother, who'd been absolutely crackers, had taken my sisters, June and Garnet, and moved away from me and my dad. As I grew older, I chafed under his brutal care and ran away from home. I went to find my sisters and was devastated to learn that Garnet had vanished three years before. Unbelievably, my mom had never reported it.

I still hated her for it. June couldn't deal and neither could Cledus. So, it surprised me that he gave the detective still working my sister's case a motorbike. Maybe he did have a heart underneath it all. Maybe he did actually give a shit.

The cops were talking to Marcel and Diego. They were working the room. My time would come. Or maybe Duchesne was the one who would be asking me questions.

Diego seemed calm and, damn him, as sexy as all hell, but I saw him wincing a couple of times. That was as much as he seemed willing to give in to an injured leg. He didn't need to prove himself as the gang's sergeant at arms by fighting Franklin the way he did, but it sure would give his street cred a bump.

Then came a new shock. Jerry, AKA Spider, the former leader of my defunct gang, Death Proof, strutted up, accompanied by his mom.

*Sue Ellen's a pistol, and she has one, too.*

*He carries it for her. And her purse.*

We locked glances. He didn't look that great, but then he'd almost gotten himself fatally gutted in a bar brawl in Austin, Texas. Diego saved his life and Jerry wound up in two different hospitals receiving treatment.

Sue Ellen came over and hugged me. Her hair was so heavily sprayed that its ends were as sharp as sticks and almost took out my eye, but I kept hugging her. She's the only maternal influence I've ever known. She smelled of good, girly things and I noticed the flash smile on Diego's face as he watched us.

"I want you to find that bitch, Teresa," Sue Ellen muttered in my ear, "and kill her. For me." She leaned back, stroking my cheek, a loving smile on her face.

Her words really blew me away. As long as I've known her, she's always kept her nose out of gang business. But I understood her anguish. Her son and my best friend, Jerry, in a futile attempt to pass for straight, had picked the wrong chick to deal with. Teresa had used him, strip-mined him of his cash to furnish a huge drug operation, then tried to kill him.

On top of it, Teresa and Franklin had conspired to put out a hit on me. With his passing, would this order to kill be revoked?

I reasoned that Jerry deserved nothing less than all this chaos for trying to pass as a straight man. But I'd done nothing to deserve Teresa's wrath.

And she stole my motorbike.

As everything whirled around me, I realized Teresa was my responsibility. My debt to the gang members in my life, not to mention my family, but, man . . . I did not want to kill a woman.

*She's evil. She tried to kill me and Jerry.*

*And I owe Sue Ellen. Big time.*

All my life in the gang and I'd managed to negotiate with my brain and smart mouth. Shit. That all went to hell in a—

A nutshell landed on the tip of my boot.

I looked down, then up, and caught Nuts' gaze. A Banni member, he'd been named for his fondness for the food, not because he's crazy. Then again, maybe he is.

"Sorry." He spat his next mouthful a little farther away.

"How ya doin'?" I asked as Jerry made his way over to me and Sue Ellen. With the death of our gang, we'd both become sworn Banni.

"Doin' all right, bro. He don't look so good." He jutted his chin toward Franklin, who was being loaded on a gurney.

It was anti-climactic and horrible at the end. Franklin would have a funeral. Gang funerals are always something to witness. Talk about going out with a bang. Not that we'd have anything to do with it. I wondered if the TV news reports would cover it. Probably. The media was fond of describing us all as 'outlaw motorbike gang members' and loved showing footage of bikers showing up for a final farewell.

My cell phone was ringing. I watched the readout. June Gold. Was she checking on me? Did she know it was all over and wanted to make sure I was alive? I hadn't really talked to her about anything significant since she, Judd, and their kids had taken up residence in Cherise's house, but I knew I'd have to deal with her at some point.

The police had finished taking everybody's statements. The paramedics transported Kennedy's body to the coroner's office. My teeth chattered as he was removed from the scene and taken away. I'd wondered how the police would view it all, but Diego had enough witnesses to prove it was self-defense.

"We'll be in touch," one of the officers said to Diego and Cledus, as I stepped away to talk to my sister.

As soon as she heard my voice, June said, "It's on TV," in a breathless tone.

"What is?" I had no idea what she was talking about.

"Franklin's murder."

I winced. "It wasn't like that—"

"No. They call it an honor killing. They say Dad is a hero. Tell him I'm baking an extra special pie for him."

*Oh, for corn's sake.* Typical of my sister. Not only is she super gullible, but food always enters a discussion, however inappropriate it might be.

"The news reports are saying there are at least seventeen unsolved homicides they couldn't arrest Franklin for, but they know it's him. No love lost there. That bastard killed my dreams and almost took my babies, too."

I hadn't noticed the news crews out front. I'd been too busy trying to be there for Diego who was, pardon the description, deathly calm.

He leaned against a wall now, looking out the window. As though he knew I was watching him, he turned and inclined his head toward me.

"We need to talk," June said. Yeah, we did. I had to tell her about my visit from the detective. We had to figure out what she'd do next. Knowing my sister, she'd want to rebuild every last brick in her bakery. It was all she had— sticky buns and her babies.

I had to press her for more details. All these years, and Duchesne and I felt she was still holding something back. "Be there soon, sis."

"I'll wait up for you."

That made me wince again. I hated family discussions with June. She became either remote or dissolved in floods of tears. Either was guaranteed to make the conversations short and not very sweet.

"Colby." Diego's soft tone cut through my sister's whining about how she wanted to talk now.

"See you soon," I said and disconnected the call. How apt was that description? I always felt like something wasn't being said when June and I talked. There was always a disconnect.

Now that Jerry was upright, he seemed to want to party. Nothing could be further from my mind—or Diego's.

"Let's go." Diego nudged me.

"I'll call you tomorrow," I told Jerry, who was already chatting away with the others. Nuts didn't look thrilled when Jerry dug his hand into his bag of pistachios, but Jerry seemed oblivious to Nuts' withering gaze.

"These are tasty," Jerry suddenly said, earning an appreciative nod from Nuts. "Mighty tasty."

"The staff of life," Nuts observed. "More people should appreciate them."

"I even love Brazil nuts." Jerry dug into Nuts' now-proffered bag.

"Me, too! Most under-appreciated nuts in the world." Nuts had found a friend. I noticed the scowl on Calvin's face—and my father's. I had a weird notion Cledus enjoyed Calvin having a boyfriend. It freed up his time some to smoke ganja and watch endless reruns of *Maury*.

"How are you on spiders?" Jerry asked, spitting a shell across the room, narrowly missing his mother's ear.

"I don't know. Never tasted one." Nuts seemed to give it some thought. "That I know of."

Jerry gave him a long look of surprise, the room went quiet, then Jerry threw his head back and laughed.

I frowned. Here were Diego and I, forced to tamp down our desire for one other and Jerry and Nuts were doing what

I supposed was the motorbike gang equivalent of flirting.

Outside, Diego and I climbed onto his Britten. I caught his grimace as he hoisted his leg over.

"Does it hurt bad?"

"I've hurt worse," he mumbled.

We strapped on our helmets. I couldn't wait to have a legitimate reason to wrap my arms around his waist. He gave a funny kind of jump as I squeezed him tight, and he turned around.

"What are you doing?"

"Hanging on for the ride."

"And what the hell's going on with Jerry and Nuts?"

I shrugged. "I think they like each other."

"Oh for . . . Next, you're gonna tell me they're going steady." He kick-started the bike. The explosion of sound almost deafened me, silencing all thought of talking.

Diego rode smoothly through the darkened streets, house lights appearing in a few places, heads peering out of windows at the unusual sound of the bike.

We arrived at what I soon realized was an alleyway behind his shop. He stopped a few doors down from the rear entrance and turned off the supersonic engine.

"Let's wheel her in," he whispered. Somewhere a dog howled. Everyone was a critic.

We hopped off the bike and pushed her up the pebbled driveway. The shop was dark, and when we got the chopper inside, Diego flipped on a single light, dropped to his knees with a couple of rags and began to polish her.

"Can I help?"

"Naw. I love doing this."

Yeah, I could tell. He was practically making love to that thing. The silence that fell between us was amiable enough, but I didn't want silence. I wanted noise. Not the motorbike variety, but the kind that only two men who are hot for each other can make. I got to my knees beside him.

"What are you doing?" he finally asked, when it became obvious I was breathing right down his neck.

"I like polishing. I'm very good at it. Want me to show you?"

He stopped rubbing and turned to me, slitty-eyed. "We talked about this, remember? We agreed we'd give it a rest for a while."

"You said it; I went along with it. Doesn't mean I like it. Do you like it?"

"Yes. No. I mean. Stop that. We agreed."

"No. Like I said, I went along with it."

"Pretended to, you mean."

"Right." I grabbed for him, and he batted my hand away.

He shook a rag at me. "You're stubborn, you know that?"

"Persistent."

"Stubborn."

I sighed. "You say tomay-toes. I say tomah-toes."

"Isn't the next line in that song something about calling it off?"

I frowned. "You're an ass. You know that?"

He lifted a brow at me. "Is that supposed to be a turn-on?"

"I don't know. Is it?"

"No," he snapped. He rubbed his bike a bit more.

I waited a bit and moved my hand to his crotch.

He stopped and looked down.

"I think you're turned on now."

He shook his head. "You're like a little kid. I bet you used to open all your Christmas presents days before you were supposed to."

"I still do." I made fast work of his zipper, and I heard his breath catching in his throat.

"Lock the door," he rasped.

I scuttled over.

"Turn off the lights, Colby."

I followed his orders and almost knocked him and the Britten over on my way back. The bike's chrome fixtures caught the moonlight. It cast a silvery light over us that felt sexy and yet, surreal. Talk about a seduction. I went for the kill, lips and hands warring over the prize package leaping for my attention.

When I pushed him onto his back, Diego threaded his hands in my hair. He bucked and rolled underneath me but soon pushed me away.

"No," he said. "Stop."

The man had nerves of steel. His cock was hard and anxious for release. He pushed me off him, rubbing at his leg.

My mouth already missed him. He got up with some effort and shoved himself away from me. I lay on the floor panting, savoring the few precious beads of juice on my tongue.

"Let's go," he rasped, shoving his cock inside his jeans. It didn't look comfortable, but then, neither was I.

My sister had been baking. I detected pecans and white chocolate on the air as Diego, and I walked into the house. It felt as though everybody else was asleep. The place was quiet.

Wordlessly, she greeted me with a hug, stared at Diego for a moment and, as if it were an afterthought, reached out and grabbed him into her bosomy embrace.

I think Diego liked it. He especially liked that she fussed over him, handing him a cup of sweet tea, saying sugar was good for shock. She cut him the first slice of pie and gave him a generous helping of whipped cream on top of it. His eyes lit up like a little kid's.

He sat on one of the barstools lined up at the breakfast bar and spooned some into his mouth. "Mmm . . . what's in the cream? I'm normally not much of a cream guy, but this is delicious." He took another bite.

My sister beamed. "Bourbon, vanilla, sugar, and a touch of rose water essence."

I sat beside him. We each wolfed down two slices, leaving nothing but crumbs on the foil pie plate. Diego gave it a longing look.

"I'll make some more tomorrow," she said. Something in her gaze seemed to signal to Diego that she wanted time alone with me.

"Well," he said, draining his tea, "I'll say good night then." He gave me an appraising glance and slid off his stool.

I wanted to ask where he was going. He lifted his hand in farewell and walked out of the kitchen. The soft thrum of a TV soon punctuated the quiet of the house.

"Everything okay?" I asked June. What a stupid question. Everything was not okay. She'd lost almost everything, and Franklin was dead. It was an honor killing, one which didn't seem to upset her at all. I looked at her long and hard as she cleaned up, carefully sponging the pie plate. She didn't resemble our mother, Evangeline, the lithe, blond, wispy-willow of a woman who'd gone insane when we were kids.

But she had a streak of Evangeline's steeliness to her.

June had dark hair, an ample figure—thanks to a lifetime spent cooking, baking, and taste-testing everything—but she wasn't fat. I thought she was a gorgeous woman. Her husband Judd's okay. Her kids, Garnet, aged four, and Henry, three-and-a-half, have Evangeline's hair and blue eyes but are loved way more than me and my sisters ever were.

Garnet and Henry had just about my whole heart, with room on the side for Diego. I dreaded anything happening to them, and I picked my moment.

"There's something I need to tell you," I said.

"What? You're gay?" She gave me a grin. "Bit late, babe. I see the way you and Diego are with each other."

I scowled at her. My sexuality was no big secret and why was she making jokes? Sometimes she worried me. I feared she'd drift off into the same Never-Never Land that had claimed Evangeline.

"Only kidding, Colby." She laid a hand on my arm. "What's going on?"

I tried to assemble my thoughts. I had to step lightly with June, but now things were moving forward again with Garnet. She had to know.

"Well, I want to discuss the bakery. I mean, your future and—"

"Oh. Is that all? Well, I intend to rebuild. The damned fire might have been a godsend actually. We can build a bigger place. As for a discussion? End of."

Her mouth had set into a hard line. Maybe she thought I'd be giving her an argument. Not likely. I'd always supported June emotionally, not to mention financially. She looked like she might walk away, so I placed a restraining hand on her arm.

"There's something else."

"Oh?" This time I saw hesitation in her eyes. "What is it?"

"I had a visit from Detective Duchesne."

She gave an exaggerated sigh. "That man gives you false hopes and—"

"No, he doesn't. I met with him, and he asked me to sign papers allowing his department to authorize two graves being dug up. They're what they call Jane Doe graves. He thinks one of them might be our Garnet."

"Where are these graves?"

The question surprised me. I don't know why. A needling doubt I'd long held began to turn into a bigger one.

53

She knew something.

"One's in Alabama. The other's in Georgia. The reason he feels one of them could be her is she matches the physical description. Both graves have been there a long time." I paused. I hadn't quite figured out how to formulate the next bit, but it mattered. Garnet Beauty mattered.

"The cops working these cases across the country have, according to Duchesne, been bothered all these years by the missing girls they have. Somebody knew and loved each one of them. Duchesne, as you know, always considered Garnet the one that got away. He hasn't forgotten her. Not one of these detectives can live with the knowledge that these babies are in anonymous graves."

She lowered her gaze, her eyelashes fluttering. She seemed like she might cry. Elbows on the countertop, she first scratched at an imaginary spot on the ancient Formica. She balled her fist, holding it to her mouth. Head down, she stared holes into the kitchen countertop.

I kept my tone soft, and I hoped, coaxing. "He's gone to great lengths to help us, June."

Her body began to sway back and forth in an agitated fashion.

I kept at her. "One of the girls, the one found in Alabama, was only discovered five years ago. Her decomposed body was stuffed inside a water cooler and tossed deep in some woods." I let that sink in a moment.

She showed signs of acute distress.

"A cooler?" When she lifted her gaze again, tears just fell down her face.

I nodded. I left out the part about the police sketch artist's face looking nothing like Garnet.

And waited.

Seconds went by, then a minute. I'd almost given up when she said, "Why did you have to sign papers?"

I tried hard to swallow my disappointment. "The various states are happy to exhume these bodies but need permission from the families that might be involved."

"Are we expected to pay for these . . . exhumations?"

It disgusted me to no end that Cledus had asked me the same question.

"Does it matter? You know I will take care of it."

"But are we?" she persisted.

"I don't know. I didn't ask." It was an effort not to display any sign of anger, even though I wanted to shake her shoulders and scream at her.

"There's something I never told you."

I said nothing. For so long I'd waited for some nugget. Some sign that she would reveal what she knew, and Duchesne and I longed to find out.

"I was afraid before, and I'm sorry I didn't tell you." Her tears flew like a torrent, splashing the countertop.

Hardly able to breathe I said, "It's okay." Even though it wasn't.

"She treated Garnet real bad."

I had guessed that much. Why else would Evangeline never have reported our baby girl gone?

My sister swiped at her tears with the backs of her hands, but more came. "I still feel guilty because . . . because . . ." She looked up at me, her face a mask of grief—pure and utter desolation.

"Evangeline used to keep her in a cage."

# CHAPTER FOUR

I have no idea how long we both sat there, but I couldn't handle the despair I felt when she told me that. I was crushed. I wanted to strangle Evangeline with my bare hands.

"Fuck," I said finally.

My sister sobbed for a long time. I didn't let her off the hook though. She told me Evangeline hated Garnet and kept her in a dog cage.

"She never held her. When Evangeline left the house, I'd take Garnet out and hug her and kiss her. She was bone thin. I'd feed her, but not too much. I was afraid Evangeline would kill me, too."

"How did Garnet react?"

"She cried a lot. She got beat real bad though when she made too much noise. Then . . ." June's voice faltered. "She stopped wanting me to touch her. She just lay on her side and slept."

I hated June. In that moment, I hated her as much as I hated my parents. I hated them all.

"Why didn't you fucking tell somebody?" I asked. There was no disguising the contempt I felt for her now.

"But I did," she said, looking surprised.

"Who did you tell?"

A long silence, then, "I told Dad."

My jaw fell open. I never thought such a thing was possible, but my whole body went slack. All these years and that bastard Cledus had known of Garnet's abuse. He'd acted shocked when I ran away from home to find the girls and discovered Garnet missing. He'd come to the house and beaten me — savagely.

And then he'd called the cops.

I had questions but couldn't say a word to her. I was angry and filled with a sense of desolation I didn't think I'd ever be able to shake off.

"He talked to Mom, and she denied everything," my sister went on. "She accused me of lying. And then one day Garnet was just . . . gone."

I couldn't look her in the eye. I left June in the kitchen and walked outside. I knew for certain my baby sister was dead. I walked and walked, weeping with grief for Garnet who hadn't deserved what happened to her. How long had she been kept a prisoner?

For hours, I stumbled, moving on, narrowly missing getting hit by a truck. The night was dark and seemed wet. I thought I was going mad.

And I'd been worried about June . . .

I stopped at a street corner, looking down at my shoes, surprised to see they were drenched. I stared at them, remembering how Garnet and June had loved *Mary Poppins*. I'd watched it recently with my niece, and she'd loved the movie, too. I'd longed for a magical, maternal figure that would come and make everything practically perfect in every way.

Spit spot, as Mary Poppins would say.

Except I couldn't move. I kept thinking about my darling girl in a cage, no longer wanting to be held. Why? What had happened to her that she'd lost the need for love?

I began to cry again. Helpless. Hopeless. Wretched.

A pair of arms came around me from behind.

"Get out of the way of the sprinklers," a voice said at my ear.

Diego.

I let him push me away from the corner. It took me a moment to realize I'd been standing outside an old plantation house that to my recollection was rumored to be haunted.

"Did you know that when they made the movie *Mary Poppins*, the author demanded the color red not be allowed anywhere in the movie?" I asked.

"No. I didn't." He took my hand and dragged me down the street.

I couldn't stop blubbering as we plodded on. He suddenly stopped, pulled me into his arms, and held me. He said nothing, but I started to calm down.

"What did she tell you?" His voice was so filled with concern, and he was so warm and lovely, I almost started falling apart again.

I pushed myself away from him. "I can't." The idea of repeating it all filled me with horror. The images dancing in my head would never leave.

"If anyone ever touches my niece and nephew, I'll kill them," I said.

"And I would help you."

In the dark of the night, I believed him. His grave eyes stared into mine. A sudden chill enveloped me. I looked to my left and almost fell over. The ghost of a woman in a wedding dress moved right beside us. She was wringing her hands as she tore through the gates of what I now realized was still the plantation property.

She disappeared halfway up the long driveway.

"Did you see what I just saw?" he asked me.

"Yeah. I saw her."

"If I'd been alone, I would have convinced myself I was imagining things." He gave me a small, sad smile. "Guess it's that kind of night."

He took my hands in his, squeezed them, and dropped them again. "Tell me."

And I did.

He said nothing for the longest time. He just kept staring at me. Diego didn't look at me when he said, "So your old man knew."

"Looks like it."

"You'll have to tell the cop."

I shook my head vehemently. It had fucked me up enough telling him.

"Come on. I'll tell him." He gestured to my pocket, and I handed him my cell phone.

"I got him on speed dial. Rogan Duchesne."

He lifted a brow. "Should I be jealous?"

That got me laughing for the first time in quite a while.

"You can be if you like."

He reached out two fingers and playfully slapped my chin.

"Ouch," I deadpanned.

He scrolled through the numbers and found Duchesne. He made the call and moved away from me as though he knew hearing him repeat the foul things I'd already said would make me go bonkers. I leaned against the rustic wrought-iron gates surrounding the plantation. So much misery. I thought of the slaves and what they'd endured. I tried not to picture Garnet in captivity, even as the question kept ricocheting in my brain.

*Why? Why? Why?*

Why had Evangeline hated her beautiful little girl so much?

Then I remembered a random, odd conversation she'd had with Cledus once. We'd all gone to the county fair. She often liked to tell people she was once the Stonewall Peach Queen. She still had the sash, and it was the only thing she fought to keep clean.

We'd gone to the State Fair in Dallas, Texas. It was the first and last time we'd gone somewhere as a family. My grandpa had become ill and couldn't attend, so my parents had gone in his place to promote his peaches. Evangeline had made three dishes with the fruit, including a pie recipe that had always won her first prize back in the day. I can't remember what happened and why she'd lost, but until this moment I'd forgotten what she said to my father.

Her exact words came back to me in very sharp focus: "It's hard for me not to be the prettiest girl in the room anymore."

Garnet was the family's real beauty—prettier, sweeter, and with the most sunny disposition. I realized now she'd been punished for that reason.

Caged.

Because she was the prettiest girl in the room.

I started to sway with the shock of this new knowledge. I hated Evangeline more than ever—and Cledus. Well, I'd pretty much given up on him a long time ago, but now I was disgusted. I wouldn't tell him what I knew. I'd let Duchesne handle the chips.

And let them fall where they may.

Diego came back to me, a troubled look on his face. "This has been one hell of a crappy night, hasn't it?"

I nodded.

"Lemme buy you a drink." He handed me back my cell phone and turned at the next corner. I trotted to keep up with him. He kept scowling. I didn't blame him. I was doing plenty of it myself.

The noise and laughter of the nightclubs around us was jarring after the total stillness we'd left behind. He led me through the back entrance of what I soon realized was his club, Artificial Moonlight. I spotted a beautiful woman, who

I felt sure was a transvestite, on the stage, speaking of artificial moonlights. Dressed in a catchy spun-gold dress, she was singing 'Autumn Leaves,' which only worsened my already morbid state.

"Wait here." Diego shoved me into a room and locked me in it. It was a small office space. I had a feeling it might be his. There was a narrow daybed in one corner and pictures of motorbikes on all the walls. I stared at his desk. An old-fashioned desktop computer that looked ready for the Smithsonian, plans galore of bikes and engines, numerous coffee cups with half-drunk liquid inside them and — the door flew open. He walked back in, a bottle of bourbon in one hand, two shot glasses in the other.

I parked my ass on the edge of the bed. He sat in his swivel chair.

He dumped the glasses on his desk and filled them. "This'll make you feel better." He slid one over to me without spilling a drop.

"Don't bet on it," I said, but downed it anyway. He swallowed his as well. The liquid fire swamped my system, but the pain in my soul was still acute.

We each downed a second shot. Damn, it was good.

He shook his head as if to ward off the effects of the bourbon. "You know, we gotta get home." He eyed the wall clock.

"Why?"

"Low profile, remember?"

"The city is asleep."

"But our enemies never do."

Shit. We resisted the urge for a third shot, until I said, "I'll split one with you."

"Fuck, Colby." He sloshed more liquor into the glasses and this time it felt good. The gnawing in my heart and body slowed.

We walked home, avoiding sprinklers and female ghosts.

The bride we'd spotted must have been on Diego's mind too, because he suddenly said, "You aren't intending to do anything stupid, are you?"

"Meaning?"

"In regards to Teresa."

I glanced at him. "Guess I can't keep any secrets from you."

"It was your dad's idea. He put it in Teresa's head, you know. Anyway, you can't do anything without the backing of the Club. You do know that."

Now I should have seen that coming, but it still pissed me off.

"I didn't say I was doing anything, okay?" My tone was harsher than I intended.

"But you have fantasies on the subject?"

I couldn't help laughing. I was more than a little drunk. "I'm thinking poison is my best option. Quick and painless. My dad's a rat bastard doing this to me."

"It's not going to happen, Colby." He gave me a dangerous look.

"I can dream."

"Your dad is jealous of you," Diego suddenly said.

"Of me? Why?"

He shrugged. "People like you. They don't like him. He's a sad old man trying to look all macho. I don't think the cops believe he killed Franklin."

"I wish they'd arrest him for something. I really hate him now."

He said nothing for a moment, then he grinned, "So, what kind of poison?"

"I don't know. Guess I'll have to read up on it."

"Something untraceable," he said.

"Yeah."

He was playing along like it was a joke. I let him think it was.

"You wouldn't do it with relish, would you . . . actually be excited about it?"

I bristled.

"Of course not. We're talking about taking a person's life." That much was true.

"A person who is a jerk, and who wants you dead. This would stop the bounty on your hide."

Dang. So, it was still active then.

"You had any more ideas about how you'd do it?"

A chill ran down my spine. "No."

"It should be quick and painless. You aren't the type to torture her for hours." He glanced at me. "Are you?"

"Of course not. What do you take me for?"

"Your old man has a thirst for violence."

"Tell me about it. I experienced it firsthand."

"Listen, if anything is to happen, the Banni will decide. Even if we give the okay for you to do it, it would have to be given some serious thought. With the gang funeral for Franklin coming up, we'll be visible. As soon as the TC get the okay to hold the funeral, most likely two to three days, any assassin will have a field day looking for you."

I hadn't really thought about that much, but it was true.

"On the other hand . . ." He gave me a grin. "Maybe everyone will be so liquored up, they'll forget about the hit. Have you ever seen anyone party the way bikers do at funerals?"

"Sure," I said. "Well, I didn't see them, but I heard all about 'em. My dad's kin, John Young, was a seaman who became the trusted advisor of King Kamehameha the Great, the first ruler of all the united Hawaiian Islands. He was a tough king who imposed harsh rules on his subjects, especially the women. They weren't allowed to eat practically anything. They couldn't eat fish, meat, or bananas . . . except at funerals. And these funerals went on for days—nonstop food and sex."

"Must have been some party back then."

"Yep."

He turned from me and fired up his computer. I was surprised it worked so fast. When I commented, he grinned.

"It's a brand-new computer built into old-fashioned housing. The guy I got it from also converts old portable typewriters into laptops."

"That sounds cool."

He started working on the computer. "So, do your fantasies involve shooting or stabbing Teresa?"

"No way. Guns are noisy, and a knife is too personal."

"But it would be poetic, don't you think? I mean she did hire goons to stab you and Jerry."

"No." I sat up straighter on the bed. "Maybe the poison angle would work. Maybe there's something we can use that will seem natural and won't tie it to the Banni." I was thinking about me, not the Banni, but he didn't have to know that. "What about deadly nightshade?"

"Yep. A possibility. The berries are deadly. We could make her eat them. It would be just like *The Hunger Games* without the love story." He snapped his fingers. "You know, if we could just find a poison to slip into her tea or coffee canister—or something."

"Hey, how about a poison dart frog?" He pointed to his screen. I saw an image of a black frog with white and yellow squiggly lines running over its body. "Oh. Their venom is harmless. Poison dart frogs bred in captivity have a low toxicity level because they're not fed the alkaloids they can get living in the wild. What a shame."

He looked so disappointed. "Hey, if we could get a golden dart frog to her, one of those has enough poison to kill twenty men."

"Bet she survives it though. That woman is Teflon tough."

He turned and looked at me, laughing. Oh, man. He was so hot. If I couldn't turn him on, making him laugh was my second-best seduction. Not that we were doing that . . .

As he went from site to site, I got up and looked over his shoulder, reading some of the more outlandish methods used to poison people.

"Some folks just have too much time on their hands, don't they?" Diego shook his head. "Listen to this. A king in ancient Persia killed his most trusted advisor by scaphism."

I peered at the screen. "And what's that when it's at home?"

"The man was tied up in a boat, naked, and force-fed milk and honey for days. When he um . . . defecated, he attracted insects," Diego said. "They stung him up and ate him alive. The whole, torturous process took seventeen days."

We stared at each other as the horror of this kind of death hit us.

"Knowing my luck, the bitch would survive that, too," I said.

Diego laughed.

"Here's one." I pointed to the screen. "Peach seeds are deadly. Peach seeds." I sat on the edge of the bed again. The more I thought about it, the more I liked it. Peaches had been the bane of my family's existence, and now Teresa was right up there with the fruit.

"Hmm . . . a novel approach. However, the poison — which is cyanide, by the way — is contained in the pit. She'd have to eat a boatload of 'em for it to work."

I fantasized about grinding the seeds and asking my sister to make them into a pie. Would Teresa eat a pie my sister made?

Oh, man. Would I even involve my sister? I shook my

head, disabusing myself of this notion. Diego's cell phone rang. He checked the readout.

"You have a family emergency," he said. "Let's book."

"What emergency?"

"Your niece woke up and won't go back to sleep."

I couldn't resist a smile. "I suppose that means sex is out of the question? A quickie would suffice, you know."

"You're bad—bad, bad, bad. You know that's off limits."

I shrugged. "I know."

We raced back to his mom's house, and this time the emergency was one I could deal with. Garnet had woken up from a nightmare and had begun crying for me. She'd woken everybody, even Nuts, who grumped, "I need my beauty sleep, goddamn it."

I apologized for Garnet. Her brother, Henry, who dotes on her, was trying valiantly to stay awake for her, but he would have settled down easily, otherwise. I went back to the kids' room where they were sharing a bed. I got between them, the adorable Henry falling asleep in my arms instantly. Little Garnet looked up at me.

"Unca Colby, I'm scared."

"Of what, baby?" I kissed her dark little head of hair. She felt warm and moist, feverish.

She burrowed her face in my neck.

"Tell me, Garnet." Saying her name was my salvation and my immense sorrow. So like her beautiful aunt. I lived in terror of something happening to her—or Henry. I became aware of my sister at the door. The watchful expression on her face made me apprehensive.

"Enough now, Garnet. Get to sleep," she said, her tone so brusque it surprised me. The little girl stiffened against me.

"Let me read you something." I leaned across her and picked up the book that lay on her bedside table.

"Not that one, this one," she said in her tiny, sweet voice, pointing to her backpack on the chair a few feet away from the bed.

"What's wrong with *Corduroy*?" I asked. "Everybody loves *Corduroy*."

She looked up at me. "It's a baby book, and I'm not a baby."

"Yes, you are," I whispered.

"No, I'm not," she whispered back.

I kissed her forehead. "I can't move. If I do, I'll wake up Henry. Want to grab the book for me, old lady?"

She giggled, shot out of bed and rifled through her backpack, returning with *The Olden Days*, a soft-covered book featuring a family in old-fashioned clothing riding a horse and buggy. She handed it to me.

As she got back into bed with me, she asked, "Were you alive in the olden days, Unca Colby?"

She snuggled into me as I leafed through the pages.

"It's set in the nineteenth-century, so no, I wasn't alive then."

"Are you sure?"

I glanced down at her. "Listen, you. It's a good thing everybody in the house is asleep—" I broke off, hearing a strange sound. I closed my eyes. Man, did Nuts chew and spit even when he was in bed? "Otherwise, I'd be tickling you," I told her.

"Tickle me, Unca Colby."

"Tomorrow."

She knew I was good for my promises and snuggled back into me as I began reading softly to her.

I didn't get very far. I'm not sure who fell asleep first, but at some point in the small hours of the morning, my sister was standing over me, shaking me roughly. I opened my bleary eyes and stared up at her. She crooked her finger, beckoning me out of the bed. I hated leaving the kids.

Garnet turned over as I got off the bed. Henry was like a dead weight, the tiny little angel boy. He didn't budge an inch.

When I finally joined my sister in the hallway, my shoulders ached, and my head pounded. I needed sleep.

I followed her into the kitchen. "What is it?" I whispered.

"What are you going to do about Teresa?"

Man, the people in my life were bloodthirsty lately.

"I've given it some thought."

"What about some action, Colby? I want her dead." She looked so flinty-eyed it made me nervous.

"I'm working out how to do it. I have to keep a low profile. I don't have the backing of the Banni yet, but I'm not about to wait."

She ignored that part. She had no idea what shit I'd be in when Chase found out—if he found out—I'd gone ahead without the action being voted on.

"What's to work out?" she demanded. "You walk up, shoot her between the eyes, and the Banni will feed her to the alligators."

I began to sweat. "The Banni are not involved yet. I'm thinking about poison."

Why, oh why, did I have to go say that?

"Poison?" Her eyes glowed like a Japanese nuclear power reactor. "Now, that's interesting. Which one were you thinking of?"

"Well, to be honest, I was thinking peach seeds but—"

"Peach seeds? Colby, do you want to give her a few minutes in the bathroom or do you want to kill the bitch? I can slip poisons into a pie nobody would ever expect. I just have to figure out how to get her to eat it. She's one of those mung bean queens."

"How do you know what she eats?"

"Don't think poison hadn't occurred to me before. I had

in mind a few scattered poisonous leaves in her salad. That might work."

She looked so excited about her new project I felt scared to ever bite into one of her pastries again. "Sis, sometimes you scare me."

June Gold beamed at me. "Thank you!"

I hadn't meant it as a compliment.

She grabbed me all of a sudden, her nails digging into my arms. "I'll give you the tools but get it to her before Kennedy's funeral. I hear there's a target with your name all over it for that day. Unless you get rid of her before then, me and Judd, we're taking the kids away someplace you'll never find us." June Gold gave me a cold, hard stare. "And don't think for one moment that I don't mean every word I say."

I had no doubt she had every intention of following through. I couldn't sleep after having this discussion and sat at the kitchen breakfast bar, looking out of the windows, watching the sun rise. A couple of times I heard noises outside and wondered if gang snipers had come looking for me.

Which would be worse—not seeing my kids again or death? The question haunted me until my eyes began to drift shut. I was awoken sometime later, light streaming into the kitchen windows.

"Here's your salad," my sister said, dumping a plastic bag in front of me. "The mung bean queen eats lunch every day before noon. I have it on good authority she never eats after five o'clock."

I nodded. I'd get it done. I had to.

"Buck up, sunshine." She clapped a hand to my shoulder. "And grow a pair."

There wasn't much I could say to that. She blew out a sigh.

"I'll make coffee."

"Thanks."

She said nothing to me as she moved around the kitchen like she owned the joint. She lent me Henry's Spider-Man backpack, and I stowed the bagged salad into it. I had no idea which were the fatal green leaves, nor did I want to. I grabbed my cell phone and stuffed it into my pocket. I drank two cups of coffee but declined toast. God knew what she might have slipped in the butter.

I left the house after she ignored my goodbye. I walked into the shop and found Diego hard at work already.

"You're awake," he said, barely looking up. "Do you know you snore like an old basset hound?"

"Thank you very much."

He looked up at me. When I caught his gaze, I asked, "You got a hog I can borrow for the day?"

Diego leaned back on his haunches, flicking a glance from my kiddie backpack to my face. He sighed. "Where you going?"

"Just for a ride. No worries."

He studied me. "All that talk when we were drunk . . . Colby, you know . . ."

"I know. Just talk, man."

Diego was still eyeing me. The man must have been psychic. Did he know or not? If he did, he wasn't saying.

I felt crappy, but I had to do what I had to do.

He slapped a set of keys in my hand. "Take my Harley that's out on the driveway. She's all gassed up and ready to roll."

Maybe he wasn't psychic. Maybe he'd been talking to my sister and knew everything. The question was, would he protect me if the Banni found out what I'd done?

"Thanks," I said.

"Funeral's tomorrow," he said, his voice quiet.

Another reminder to get it done today. I said nothing. I resisted the petty urge to say *what the fuck ever.*

"Thanks again."

"Keep it stiff," he said to my retreating back. I pretended not to hear him, but he made me smile. Lucky for him I had places to go, people to poison.

It hit me that I had no idea where Teresa was. I'd been to her home in Austin, but my sister had mentioned she had a farm in Baton Rouge. That gave me pause, and then I remembered.

There was a community garden near Louisiana State University, and Teresa and Jerry had taken over a small portion of one from a family who'd sold their share on Craigslist. Jerry had a bungalow near the gardens but still spent time at his mom's house. Jerry just couldn't be alone. I wondered if Teresa was staying at the house on Woodwick Lane.

I hadn't been there since Teresa had become a fixture in Jerry's life. She'd put so much pink and lace stuff in the joint it made me shudder. Jerry had a hard time being there, too. He often went to his mom's just to get some peace and quiet — and a little less macramé.

The wind whipped my face as I took off on the hog, and I felt better than I had for days. Riding a bike was freedom. Riding was my life. My pa once said the most dangerous risk of all is spending life not doing what you want. He's so right.

It took me twenty minutes to get to Woodwick. I stashed the chopper behind some bushes at a house that had a for sale sign on it that looked like it had been hanging there a while. I got off the bike, removed my helmet, mindful that Pa believed it to be a useful weapon. I saw no motorbikes and no sign of life, save for a tethered dog on a porch. He didn't look happy, and I didn't blame him.

I took my time getting down to number seventeen. I almost fell over. Jerry's Corvette was in the driveway. It had disappeared after he'd been wounded in Austin. Diego and I had been pretty certain she'd taken it, and Jerry's signature custom bike made to look like a huge, silver spider. He'd left my Harley at her property in Austin, and that had vanished, too, along with Jerry's collection of vintage bikes.

Cutting down the neighbor's side of what looked like a new wooden fence, I strapped the helmet to my backpack and climbed up a corner bough of a leafy walnut tree. Once I found a solid perch, I dragged out the binoculars. I focused on the back part of Jerry's cottage.

It was almost too good to be true. She was in the kitchen, chopping vegetables and salad fixings. And, oh holy crap, she had no top on. Her boobs were huge and almost anatomically improbable—just too damned perky.

She moved away, and I couldn't see her anymore. I waited, and she came back, a tomato in her hand. She chopped away and then moved from the window once again. I took my chances and jumped over the fence, landing in her asparagus patch, clunking my leg with the helmet. Cledus was right. The damned thing hurt.

I rolled out of the patch. Thank God she wouldn't live long enough to see the mess I'd made of her neat little rows. I didn't pay the vegetables much mind. I stayed low to the ground and made a run for the back door.

I could hear the sound of clicking. High heels. I waited a moment and crept around the side of the house. A vacuum cleaner. I bobbed up to peer through the window.

*My eyes! My eyes!* She was vacuuming stark, staring naked in nothing but high-heeled red shoes.

I dropped to the ground. The sound droned on. It moved away from the window, and I moved back around toward the kitchen. That's when I saw it.

Jerry's spider bike, painted bubblegum pink, lay against the garage door. A Barbie doll sat on the edge of the seat, a big plastic spider stuck to her face. Jerry would freak. I dropped down low again and took a quick photo with my camera phone. I straightened, stayed against the kitchen door, and peered into the window. She was still vacuuming, by the sound of things, and her salad was sitting in a huge bowl on the kitchen countertop.

I put the backpack on the ground, left the binoculars I'd brought along next to it, and took the salad out of the backpack. I prayed the back door was unlocked and turned the handle. It was. Thanking God for the noise covering any sounds I inadvertently made, I grabbed handfuls of my salad and mixed it in with hers, transferring some of her stuff loose into my backpack.

Uh-oh. The vacuum went off, just as I was putting some of her original leaves on top of the pile in the bowl.

I heard her talking to somebody. Did she have company? Then the vacuum started up again as I quickly closed the door. A hand clamped over my mouth and another to my shoulder. I screamed anyway and turned to find Jerry standing there.

"Shh," he muttered. "What are you doing here?"

He knew. He already knew.

"You gonna be quiet?" he whispered.

I nodded again. He dropped his hand then pointed over his shoulder toward the bike. "Did you see what she did?"

He pulled a gun out.

"No need for that," I told him. "Poison . . ." I moved my head in the direction of the house. "In the greens."

He smiled. "I can't wait for her to eat herself to death. I want to mess her up."

"Don't," I implored.

The vacuum went off, and she stomped back in the kitchen, a male voice arguing with her.

"We're eating salad," she said, in an insistent tone.

"I don't eat salad." I stole a glimpse through the window

before Jerry, and I dropped down.

*Holy. Fucking. Shit.*

It was Chase. As in, the leader of the Banni.

Why, that dirty, double-crossing, two-bit hustler. Here was my father taking the fall for him, and Chase was over here balling Barmy Barbie.

"You'll eat my salad," she chirped, "if you want to get near this pussy again."

Eee-eeww!

She was moving about now, fussing at him to get a couple of plates.

"You've never tried anything like this, as long as you've lived," she said.

Next thing we heard was their noisy kissing.

*Oh, geez.*

"Whatever you say, sweet cheese." Chase sounded so much happier. I wondered what the hell he was doing here with her. And, oh crap, the Banni would go bonkers if Chase died, even if he was obviously some treacherous kind of bastard. If Teresa was in league with the TCs, what excuse did Chase have for being here?

Chase and Teresa walked away from the kitchen, and I sighed.

"We can't kill Chase," I said to Jerry.

"The hell we can't!" He jabbed a thumb over his shoulder. "The Banni doesn't even know you're here, do they?"

I shook my head, but I still wasn't sure if Diego knew or not.

"Look what she did to my bike, Colby!" He grabbed at his stomach. "Not to mention me! Chase is a traitor. You think the Banni will cry over him?"

He was getting a bit vocal now, and I tried to get him to quit hollering.

Too late. Chase and Teresa were back.

She looked horrified, her big, puffy hairdo looking

ridiculous.

"What the . . ." I saw her mutter. She yanked open the door, just as Jerry whipped out a pistol from the back of his pants and shot her right in the forehead, messing up her artfully arranged curls and blowing her backward, right into Chase. He let out an "*oof* " as she landed on top of him and they hit the kitchen door. Her sightless eyes stared up, and her blood was everywhere.

Chase pushed her off him. "Fuck," he wheezed. "I thought she'd never shut up."

He got to his feet, looked at the blood spatter, and said, "Shame, really, after she bleached the shit out of the kitchen all morning." He picked up the salad bowl and emptied it all over her.

"Bon appetite, bitch," he said, dumping the bowl into the trash bin beside her.

Man, was he cold.

He looked at us.

I held my breath.

"Sorry, Jerry, but she's been bangin' everybody."

Jerry opened his mouth, but Chase held up a hand. "Let's split," he said. It wasn't a suggestion. I wiped down the door handle with my sleeve, then Jerry and I took his advice.

I was a little worried about Chase's machismo when I saw him get on the altered spider bike. He gave the Barbie doll a little pat on the head and zoomed off, leaving a trail of dust behind him.

"Well," Jerry said, "Ain't that a kick in the head?"

# CHAPTER FIVE

Diego

My mother had a doctor's appointment in the morning, so I was stuck working at the scrapyard, doing inventory with Tammy. Cherise was having some lady problems, nothing serious, she said. Something to do with menopause.

Marcel wasn't answering his phone, and that was making me anxious. I'd sent him to tail Colby, to find out what in hell he was really up to. Yes, we'd talked hypothetically about this or that. I figured he was trying to tell me something without coming right out with it. I wasn't completely convinced he was really going after Teresa. Wasn't sure Colby had it in him to kill someone, let alone a woman. But damn it, if he really was going to do that, he couldn't just ride off and put the woman in the ground without club approval. Death Proof wasn't the Banni. The Banni had rules — strict rules — and if you broke them, there were dire consequences. From what I knew of Death Proof, there seemed to be a hell of a lot more leniency.

Tammy was rubbing my arm again. She did that kind of thing when she was close. It was irritating me. All I could think about was if Colby had gone ahead and killed Teresa, I'd have to find a way to cover it up so the club wouldn't know. If no one saw him, then just maybe her death could be blamed on the TCs.

I moved away from Tammy and went to the window.

"What's wrong, Diego?" She followed me. "You all

right?"

I glanced at her. "Fine."

She moved closer. "I miss you. You hardly ever come here anymore. Your mom worries." She sighed. "We haven't been together since Mardi Gras. You seem tense. I could help you to relieve that tension."

I went back to the counter. "Tammy . . ." I looked at her. "Why don't you find yourself a nice boyfriend."

I saw the tears spark in her eyes. Damn it, I didn't fucking need this today. But in spite of the stress I was under, I walked over and gave her a brief hug. "Don't cry over me. I'm not worth it."

She touched my cheek. "I want to be your old lady. Don't you know that I love you, Diego? In fact, I'm not the only want who'd want that place. Sandy and—"

I put up a hand. "You don't love me, Tammy. You love my position in the club."

"That's not true," she snapped. "The others maybe, not me. They know one day you'll be leader of the Banni. You should challenge Chase for leadership. Why don't you, Diego?"

"I don't want to be leader."

"The others respect you, look up to you. You already are the leader in their eyes. And I could be right there at your side. Diego, I'd do anything for you." She reached for the zipper on my pants.

I pushed her hand back. "Not now. Look, let's get these books . . ." I paused as I heard the sound of a bike drive up. I went to the window. Marcel. I looked at Tammy. "Carry on with the accounting. I'll be back in a minute." I stepped out into the bright sunshine and waited impatiently for Marcel to get off the bike.

I walked over. "Hey man," I said. "So? Did you see Colby?"

"Yeah," he sighed, "and you won't believe it."

"Is Colby all right?" I almost couldn't breathe for a second.

He nodded.

I took a breath again.

"Where is he? What happened?"

"Well, I followed him like you said. He went after Teresa, just like you suspected. Then Jerry shows up. I'm not sure what they were doing in the bushes by the backdoor. Waiting, I guess."

Colby really did it. He put poison in her food.

"Jerry? What in fuck was he doing there?"

"No idea."

"Go on."

"Anyways, you'll be surprised when I tell you who Teresa was keeping company with." Marcel lifted an eyebrow, and I waited. "Chase."

"Chase? You mean Chase was banging Teresa?" I shook my head. "Oh fuck. Okay, who's dead?"

"Teresa," Marcel smirked. "Jerry shot her in the head. Then get this, Chase comes out like it's nothing, apologizes to Jerry, and says they should all hit the road. They follow Chase to some sleazy bar called Delano's, and the three of them are drinkin' like sailors on layover."

"Are they still there?" I demanded.

"I think so."

Marcel told me that they'd made a deal. Chase would keep his mouth shut about the hit, even give his approval, as long as they didn't talk about him being there with Teresa. Nice. But I was about to blow their little bargain straight out of the water.

Colby and Jerry were playing poker with the wrong gambler. I knew Chase a lot better than they did. Chase would never let anyone live who had something on him. The first chance he had to get rid of both of them, he would.

I slapped Marcel on the back. "Go and help Tammy with the bookkeeping. I'll be back soon." I walked over to my bike and got on, watching as Marcel walked into the scrapyard office. I strapped on my helmet and roared my bike to life.

I wasted no time getting to Delano's, a real hole in the ground. I wanted to be there while the three of them were still sober enough to understand what I had to say. My cell phone rang as soon as I turned off the engine. I checked the caller ID. Unknown. I flipped open my phone. "Yeah? Who's this?"

"Badger. How's it hanging, Champagne?"

"What do you want?"

"You."

"Me? The fight is over. We won. Leave it alone."

He laughed. "It's not about Kennedy. It was a fair fight. I knew you'd take him. I've seen you fight before, saw you play college ball too. You were one hell of a quarterback, could have made pro if you hadn't fucked up your knee."

"Thanks for the trip down memory lane. So, you still haven't told me why I'm wasting precious minutes listening to your shit."

"Chase wants a meeting. The grow-op is on our territory, and yet he holds the deed to the land. I hear that our dear Teresa is no longer part of the picture."

"Is that so? News must travel fast."

"You wouldn't know anything about how she got dead, would you?"

"Nope. Not a thing."

"That's the Diego we all know and love."

"Don't love me too much, Badger."

He laughed. "Well, no loss as far as that one goes, but it does mean you guys own more than your share with Jerry on board. We're not about to let you cross into our territory without a healthy cut of the profits."

"What the fuck does this have to do with me? Call Chase and negotiate. "

"I don't want to deal with Chase. He parties too hard, is unreliable and doesn't keep his word. No one in the TC club respects him. We want to deal directly with you, or it's no deal."

"I'll call you back," I said and hung up. Right now, I had more important things to do than play politics with the leader of the Texas Crushers.

I stood in front of the bar for a second, glanced at the sign hanging above the rundown building, and watched an old drunk stagger out the door. "Fucking Bikers in there," he muttered. "Watch yourself."

I grinned at him. The two tipped cocktail glasses with half the lights burnt out was swinging back and forth above my head, an accident waiting to happen. This was Delano's, the perfect place for loser drunks, and over-the-hill prostitutes, not to mention druggies and, yes, bikers.

I pushed the door open and walked in. There in the corner sat Colby, Chase, and Jerry, slamming their glasses together and looking right chummy.

When they saw me, they just stared at me and fell quiet.

"How sweet," I said, as I took a chair, turned it backward, and straddled it. I could tell they were all wasted by the goofy expressions on their faces. I stretched out my legs and looked at Chase. "When were you planning on letting me know you were banging Teresa?"

"What are you, my wife?" He had drool in his beard. It was disgusting.

"No," I said between clenched teeth. "I'm just the guy that protects your ass. It would be kinda good to know what I'm being shot at for."

"Did someone shoot at you?" Colby asked. He almost reached out to touch me then held back.

"No." I shook my head. "But they would have." I turned my attention back to Chase. "Is it possible for you to keep your prick in your pants once in a while?"

Jerry pushed his chair back. I'd caught the look of rage that crossed Chase's face.

Chase got to his feet. Colby picked up his beer and also stood.

I didn't move a muscle.

"You fucking son of a bitch," he yelled, staggering a little as he knocked over the chair.

A few other customers hightailed it out of there.

"I'll fuck you up, Diego," he threatened, baring his teeth at me. "Who in the hell do you think you're talking to?"

I looked up at him. "You really want to do this?" I asked him. I knew he couldn't take me when he was sober, let alone when he was wasted.

He pulled a switchblade out of his pocket, swearing.

I laughed. "Go ahead. Try," I told him.

He made a lunge for me. With one arm, I yanked him across the top of the chair to the opposite side of me. The table tipped over, and the pitcher of beer smashed to the floor. Colby and Jerry were now a few feet away. Chase was on the floor, and I was still sitting there.

I glanced to the side as Chase tried to get up. When he was halfway, I sprang to my feet, pulled out a pistol, put a hand on his head, and kept him on his knees. I pressed the pistol to his head.

I heard Jerry and Colby say something. I didn't pay attention.

My voice was calm when I told him, "Listen to me and listen well. I'm only going to say this once. If you ever go behind my back again—for money, for pussy, for anything—I

81

don't care what the club does to me. I will kill you. Did I make that clear?"

He nodded.

I released him and tucked the gun back into my jacket.

He leaned on the chair and rose to his feet. "Are you challenging me for leadership, Diego?"

"No. I just don't like being made a fool of."

"I'll have the club banish you, vote you out," Chase threatened. "Burn that fucking tattoo right off your hide."

"You'd be doing me a favor, but it wouldn't bode well for you," I told him.

"What do you mean?" he demanded.

"Badger just called me. The Texas Crushers don't want to negotiate the drug deal with you. They'll only deal with me."

Chase's jaw went slack.

"Still want to get rid of me?" I met his gaze and stood up.

There was silence.

"That's what I thought," I muttered and walked out.

I wasn't surprised when Colby came after me. I kept walking, and he fell in beside me.

"You had Marcel follow me," he accused.

I looked at him. "Yeah, I did."

"Why?"

"You know why."

"I told you what I'd do."

I pointed at him. "We spoke hypothetically. You're just lucky Chase was fucking that woman. Colby, you're not a free agent. You're Banni now. The club votes on shit like that. The same goes for Jerry. I suggest you counsel him."

He sighed. "Are you mad at me?"

I looked at him. "Should I be?"

"Deep down you knew, Diego," he insisted. "That's why you sent Marcel." He looked at the sidewalk.

I sighed. He was right, of course.

"I'm not happy about the babysitter." A flash of anger in his eyes ignited my own.

"Goddamn it. How many times do I have to say it? There are rules, Colby. You don't just go off and do your own thing, no matter how much it's warranted. It has to be taken to the club. That's the way it works. And Chase, that double-crossing son of a bitch. Where are his brains?"

I was ranting.

Colby started to laugh.

I stared at him. "What's so funny?"

"Now that I think about it, you were worried about me."

"It wasn't that."

"Yes, it was that," he said softly. "You thought I'd get killed."

I shook my head. "I thought that the club would find out and that Chase would . . . I didn't know the asshole was banging Teresa. If I had . . ."

"You can't tell the club he was with her," Colby said. "I made a bargain with Chase."

"Marcel knows." I sighed. "I'll have to talk to him before he tells the others. I have to go."

Colby grabbed my arm. "I'm touched you were worried, but I'm still not happy you had me followed."

"Well then, next time you get some crazy idea to play the Lone Ranger, don't tell me about it." I pointed at him. "Let the chips fall where they may."

Jerry came out and interrupted us. "Diego," he said, "Chase wants the scene cleaned up. He wants Teresa buried and—"

"Oh yeah?" I straddled my bike. "Tell him to go to the hardware store and buy a fucking shovel." I stepped on the gas and roared off down the road.

First chance I got, I pulled over and called Marcel. He was

still at the scrapyard. "You haven't seen any of the others?"

"No. What's up?"

"Don't talk about what you saw, okay?"

"Okay."

"The TCs seem cool with what went down, but they don't know about Chase being there. They only suspect it was our hit. So, there's no problem."

"Okay, boss."

I hung up. Keeping a war from exploding between our club and the TC was like walking a tightrope. If they wanted me as negotiator, they'd get me. The club could vote on it if Chase opposed, but he wouldn't. He wanted the deal; he wanted the money. That's all that counted in the end.

I was busy working the books again with Tammy an hour later. Marcel was out in the yard, waiting on a customer. The guy was looking for a custom-made hubcap. I doubted he'd locate one but, hell, one never knew what you'd find out there.

I was in the back room when I heard Tammy talking to someone, flirting really. I came out to see a disheveled Colby standing there.

"Hey." He smiled faintly at me.

"I have a question for you." Tammy interrupted before I could say hello. She was looking at Colby.

"What's your question?" he asked. His gaze was back on me again. He had this way of looking at me as if he were slowly removing my clothes. It made me feel warm all over—too damn warm.

"You think I'm beautiful, right?" Tammy glanced back at me.

"Sure." Colby shrugged. "You're very pretty." His gaze stayed on me.

"You'd be proud to have me as your ole lady, wouldn't you?"

Colby smirked. "I guess."

"Well, then tell that to your blockheaded friend here. Diego hasn't fucked me in months." She gave me a dirty look and huffed off to the stockroom.

Colby came closer. "I feel for her," he said softly. "In fact, I can identify, even if it's only been a couple of days. It sure feels like months." He met my gaze.

I looked away. "What do you want, Colby?"

"Are you mad?"

"No," I looked at him. "Stop asking me that."

"I've cooled off now. I wanted to tell you that what you did really touched me. It turns me on to think you care so much."

"Don't let it go to your head." I scoffed.

He smiled. "Okay. Listen, I need your help."

I met his gaze. "What with?"

"Chase told me to bury the body. I . . . well . . . I've never done this sort of thing and . . . I . . ." He swallowed. "Don't want to do it alone."

"I'll send someone with you," I said.

"No." He shook his head. "Please. You . . . I want you . . ." He stopped, sighing. "I just want you."

He looked upset.

"You didn't kill her."

"Doesn't matter. I went there to do the job. Ever wonder what kind of man you have to be . . . to kill? Vengeance and . . ."

"How drunk are you?" I grinned.

"Pretty wasted." He laughed.

"Why isn't Jerry helping you?"

"Chase and Jerry have passed out. They took two rooms upstairs in that dive to sleep it off. I'm the only one left standing."

I nodded. "Okay, I'll come with you. We need a vehicle

and a few things. Meet me back at the clubhouse in a half hour."

"Thanks," he said, looking relieved.

I watched him walk out, then heard the bike start up. I hoped he could stay upright on that thing, but then, I'd coddled him enough. I couldn't be seen to be too protective, although I was certainly operating under the Banni code. We protected our own.

A half hour later, I was driving what we all referred to as a disposable vehicle. After the deed, this old van would end up on the crusher in the scrapyard.

Colby was fighting sleep in the passenger seat, and I was ruminating. How did I know I'd end up stuck cleaning up the mess? *Damn you, Chase.*

I scouted for cops on the way, but it was quiet. When we got to the house, I parked around back and woke Colby.

"Oh, man, I got a hangover," he groaned.

"It serves you right." I threw him a pair of rubber gloves. "Put them on." I slipped into a pair as well.

When I walked in the back door of the house, I saw Teresa lying naked on the floor in a pool of blood. She was covered in salad. My eyes widened. I looked at Colby, who made a face. "Jesus." I sighed. "Okay, get the blanket from the van. We need to cover her up and carry her out. Then we have to clean up good."

Colby seemed a little freaked by the corpse, but with a little encouragement, helped me carry it out and place in the back of the van.

The moon was beaming in the night sky when we began to dig, far enough in the woods where no one would happen upon the grave. Colby was really hurting from the hangover, and I ended up doing most of the digging.

Finally, with relief, I tossed the final shovel full of dirt over the grave. I was soaked to the skin. Colby's heavy drinking had pretty well done him in. He practically crawled back to the van.

He didn't say much. In the vehicle, he looked at me for a minute. I wasn't sure what was going to come out of his mouth. "Diego?"

"Yeah?" I wiped sweat off my forehead.

"I need you tonight."

That wasn't what I wanted him to say.

"Colby," I warned.

"Listen. We're alone. Can't we stop somewhere on the highway for a couple of hours, a motel?" His hand crept over onto my thigh. "No one will know. You need a shower."

I covered his hand with mine and squeezed it. "Maybe they won't know," I said softly, looking into his eyes. "But Colby, don't you think that —"

"Think? Think? How in hell can I think when you're this close to me," he whispered. "My heart beats so hard in my chest, I think I'll die. I might die if I can't touch you. Please, don't tell me I can never touch you again?"

"Stop." I pulled my hand away. "You're just upset. I understand. But each time we're together . . . it's . . ." I sighed. "It's hard for me. Don't you see? We have to put time and space between us. If we don't stop coming together like this, we'll never move on."

He shook his head and looked away. "Move on? Move on to where, Diego? We can't move on, and you know it. I ache for you. I know you ache for me. I see it in your eyes." He turned to look at me. "Tell me it's a lie. Tell me you don't want me."

I swallowed. "I can't tell you that, but . . ." I started the engine. "One of us has to be strong."

"I don't want to be strong," he muttered.

I drove out onto the highway, my attention on the road. I

hated this. And of course, damn it, I was tempted. What could it hurt to spend a few hours with Colby in a motel room? I wanted to be strong, perhaps even to put this thing behind us for good. But damn it, I was only a man. I had a flash memory of Colby and me together. I could feel my cock harden uncomfortably between my thighs, and I remembered what it felt like to hold him and to fuck him. Who was I kidding? I wanted Colby desperately. Probably I even loved him. But I couldn't go there . . . not ever. Loving him would finish me.

Sex. Just sex. That's all it could be, stolen moments that no one could ever find out about.

The motel sign loomed up ahead, calling to me, tempting me. There was a vacancy sign, which meant I had no excuses left. I glanced at Colby. His hands were clenched. He looked at me as I slowed down. I drove up to the little cabins, all in a row, and stopped in front of the one marked Office.

I heard Colby sigh.

"Do you know what you're doing to me?" I asked him.

His hand moved to my thigh again. "It's nothing that you're not doing to me, baby."

"Do you know how risky this is?"

"I'd risk anything right now. I want you so much, it hurts. Please," he pleaded, meeting my gaze.

I parked the van and got out. As I headed to the office, I felt as if I were a dead man walking, heading for the electric chair somehow, and yet . . . I was happy.

I shuddered a little, thinking of what it would feel like to have this tattoo burnt off my back, to hear the sneers and the taunts, to wish for death because the pain was just too much. I remembered soon after being recruited, watching the Banni torture a guy, a traitor to the club who'd stolen some money. They chained him to the floor and did unspeakable things to him. The poor guy begged for death. If that happened to

Colby . . .

I opened the door to the office, and a man appeared, balding with glasses. I'd taken off my jacket, but I looked a fright, my T-shirt soaked to the skin, dirty.

I took out some money. "How much for two rooms? I need a shower and ah . . ." I glanced through the window at Colby, "my friend needs some sleep." Two rooms was a good idea, even if we'd only use one.

"Eighty for the two. No parties." He eyed me.

"No worries. Could we have the two at the end?"

"Sure." He pushed a registration form across the desk. "Don't get no business since they put in the new highway."

"This isn't the Bates Motel, is it?" I grinned.

He didn't get it. "What?"

"Never mind. Look, I'll give you double if I don't have to sign the form." I looked him in the eye.

"You on the run?"

"Well, only from my ole lady. Alimony. That bitch is sucking me dry. I work like a dog. Look at me. Can't get a break."

He winked. "Gotcha." He took back the form, and I handed him the money.

"Won't need nothing. Just shower and sleep."

"You won't be disturbed, young man."

I smiled and walked out with the keys in my pocket. I got back in the van and looked at Colby. His eyes were closed. He'd gone to sleep. I laughed a little. All this trouble and Colby was out like a light.

A few minutes later, I opened the room at the end and pulled Colby out of the van. He was mumbling something, and I got him in the room and laid him down on the bed. I looked down at him for a moment, and something hurt. I left him to sleep and went next door, messing up the bed. I took a shower there but had to put my dirty jeans back on. I stared out the window at the vehicle. I should take it back now, but I guess it wouldn't hurt to wait until morning.

I returned to the room where I'd left Colby and lay next him on the narrow bed. He was fast asleep. I touched his hair and kissed his temple. "Sleep, baby," I said softly, then closed my eyes.

When my eyes finally opened, I saw a stream of light peeking through the thin, ugly curtains hanging off the window beside the door. I turned my head and found myself looking into Colby's eyes. He smiled at me. "Good morning, sleepyhead," he said softly. He reached out and pushed some hair off my forehead.

"How long have you been awake?" I asked him, almost in a whisper. There was something so intimate, so sacred, about us lying here like this, even though we hadn't had sex.

I knew he felt it, too, when he answered so softly. "A while. I've been watching you sleep."

I made a face. "How exciting." I smiled.

"It was. You are so beautiful, and it's a gift, to be able to lie here beside you like this, even if I'm not touching you. I can hear you breathe, hear the little sounds you make in your sleep. You know that I love you."

That was like a punch a chest. I shook my head. I couldn't make words.

"I told you if I ever fell, it would mean I'd lose you."

The look he gave me was so intense I had to close my eyes.

"Don't," he said.

I opened my eyes. "Why?" I asked.

"I don't know. Maybe because I shouldn't. Maybe because I can't help it. And I swore it would never happen to me. So . . . a part of me resents you."

Colby sat up and rubbed his face with his hands.

I stared at him. "You drive me fucking crazy." It was the first time my voice went up in volume. "When we first met, you wouldn't stop until I came to you, wouldn't stop until you got what you wanted. Then after, you told me you didn't want it anymore. And now, when the worst possible thing would be to fall in love, you do it?"

I swung my legs over to the side of the bed, ran a hand through my hair. I had my back to him. I was shaking. "I'm not going to say it."

"Then don't," he replied. I detected urgency in his voice. Then I felt his arms come around me from behind. His lips caressed the back of my neck. "Don't say anything at all." He grabbed my shoulder and pushed me down on the bed. "Just do one of the two things that you do best, Diego Champagne—either fuck me or beat the shit outta me."

My eyes widened.

"You're not leaving this room until you make a choice." He dumped a row of condoms on the bed.

"I'd never hurt you," I told him.

His hand moved over my bare chest. "Well then, I guess your choice is clear." His hand settled at the top of my treasure trail.

I reached up and cupped my hand around his neck. His mouth lowered to mine and pressed softly against my lips that I opened to his as his need intensified. He straddled my waist without breaking contact and kissed me so hard, it hurt. He grunted, breathing hard, as he tore away from me and moved down to undo my pants. He was a man with a mission, one that wouldn't be denied, and I couldn't have stopped him if I'd wanted to. And God knows, I didn't want to.

He was on the floor, between my spread thighs and, for a moment, his bright gaze exploring my flesh like he couldn't get enough. He almost hesitated. I held out my hand.

"Touch me," I groaned. "Come on."

He landed his hands on my thighs and moved up. He pulled my legs forward and lowered his head between them. His tongue slid around the head of my cock, and it was like a jolt of electricity going through me.

I grabbed a handful of his hair and, like a drowning man grasping a raft, I held his head there. "Colby," I moaned. "Take it. Take it."

His lips surrounded my wet cock. The sounds of his ministrations were as stimulating as what his lips and tongue were doing to me. My hips lifted up, and his hands pushed me down. I almost couldn't handle it. I was going to come, and it was probably a record. There was something about touching his hair, seeing his head between my thighs, watching it move up and down as he reached for my hand. Every cell in my body seemed alive and the come shot through me like a bloody tidal wave.

He was looking at me as my knees lifted and I sat up, trembling, a cry that started at my stomach and ended in the air made him smile.

Colby took off his clothes and lay down beside me. I regained my breath and hovered over him. I began to kiss him—mouth, neck, chest, stomach—all the way down to his cock, which was standing at attention, waiting for me. I licked it, sucked, handled his balls, but I was nowhere near to satisfying it.

I was hanging on, the sounds of struggle ringing in my ear. I turned him over and pulled him onto his knees. He opened to my tongue and to my fingers as I caressed his ass, reached around to keep him hard. I pulled him up in my arms and touched him everywhere.

He moaned, said my name.

"You told me once I couldn't handle you," I reminded him with a smile.

"You know . . . why. He grunted. "I was mad at you . . . It's not . . ."

"But I'll have to redouble the effort," I teased, catching his earlobe with my teeth. I kept him back in my arms, stroked his cock straight out.

His hips began to bump back against my erection. "Fuck me," he breathed.

"In good time." I kissed the nape of his neck, slapped his erection a few times, and squeezed it. I pinched his nipples, and he squirmed against me. "Diego. Damn. I can't hang on."

"Yes, you can," I smiled. "You know what's coming."

He laughed a little, turned his head and kissed me passionately on the mouth, while I squeezed his cock. He moaned. And I pushed him down on the bed, gave him a swift smack on the bottom, and opened his ass with my fingers. I teased him some with the head of my cock, hard again and ready to take Colby exactly where he wanted to go.

He pressed his ass against my cock. I jabbed myself inside him, and Colby swore. I chuckled. "It's nice to be wanted."

"I'm going to —" He began.

I didn't let him finish. I pushed deeper, and he went slack, his head dropping. I took a breath, feeling him all around me, possessing me, and I was losing it now. The control was gone, and here I was, as weak as a kitten inside him. Big, tough Diego was nothing but Colby's slave. I grabbed the back of his neck, and my body took over, moving inside him — hard, fast, then slow, sweet torture that ripped deep inside my heart. I sped up again, and our bodies moved in a rhythm — slick, wet flesh pressed together in holy lust, forever and ever, amen. And it was amen in the holiest of ways. Inside him felt like being reborn and dying all at the same time.

It felt like the room was shaking, as we made those incoherent sounds only two men could make in the heat of it. Wet, aching, exhausted, we came together, clinging together, afraid to let go.

I came inside him hard, all the strength in me flowing away. If my enemies had wanted to kill me, I would have gladly gone to my death. I could die looking at Colby, and that would be all right somehow.

I stopped looking at him. In fact, I rolled over on the bed away from him while he sat there, his arms folded around his legs. Silence permeated a room that a few minutes ago had been filled with our ecstasy. It was time to come back to reality, one that was hard and stone cold. We couldn't touch, we couldn't fuck, and we couldn't be together.

The shower started, and I rolled over. I don't know why I couldn't look at him right now, but it was just too hard. I knew now the worst had befallen me. I'd die for Colby. I'd give my life for his, and the reason why was something I didn't even want to explore. But it was there, that word, the same one he'd had the balls to say to me a while ago. Not saying it wouldn't make it go away, but it allowed me some distance. I'd let it float around out there without naming it because my heart couldn't take it.

And when Colby walked back into the room, a towel wrapped around his waist, I knew that in spite of all his loss, out of the two of us, Colby was the stronger when it came to human emotion.

# CHAPTER SIX

I couldn't say if Colby regretted his confession of love to me or not. The silence between us on the way back to the city was ominous. He reached out for my hand at one time, and I took it. I held it in mine for a long while, and when the city came into view, I let it go.

At the scrapyard, I let Colby off, and I drove the vehicle out to what we referred to as the graveyard and left it there for the crusher. I'd take care of that later.

I walked through the piles of scrap and back to the office, where I found my mother and Colby chatting about the heavy rainstorm that we were supposed to get tonight.

"There he is." My mother pointed at me. "Where did you get to, child?"

Colby grinned. "Child?"

I gave him a sassy look. "I had an errand to run. How was the doctor's visit?"

"Oh, he gave me some medication to take, supposed to stop the hot flashes. He don't know nothin.'"

I smiled, walked over, and gave her a kiss. "I got to get to the bike shop. Where's Marcel?"

"Still in back. He's been stroking Tammy all day. What did you say to her to get her panties in a bunch?"

Colby leaned against the counter and lifted an eyebrow.

"Enjoying yourself?" I muttered.

He laughed. "What did you say to get her panties in a bunch?"

"That girl is way too sensitive." I waved a hand.

"People in love usually get that way." My mother eyed me. "When you going to make an honest woman of one of these girls? They'd all have you. Just like your father—charm and good looks. I always said they handed out too much to that man." She shook her head.

"Too bad that's all he got." Diego sneered. "Less good looks and a backbone would have been better."

Cherise looked at Colby. "Diego's father was a fighter, you know?"

Colby looked at me. "Really? Like a boxer?"

"Yes," I said, between clenched teeth.

"He could have been a champion." She sighed. "Drank a little too much. Liked to have a good time." She laughed.

"You loved him a lot, didn't you?" Colby said, walking over to my mother.

She nodded. "Yes. And every time I look at that boy over there . . ." She sniffed, wiping at her eyes. "It's a bitch to be in love like that."

I looked up, and Colby's gaze met mine. I swallowed hard and looked away. "Gotta go."

I didn't wait. I got on my bike and rode. Whenever I needed to escape, this was it. Damn it. I didn't want to hear about my old man. When I'd needed him, he was gone. He never cared a damn about me or my mother. How could she still love him?

Several of the members were at the clubhouse. I hailed two of the grunts, Danny and Storm, and told them to go to the scrapyard. "Make sure there's nothing left of that vehicle," I said. "Is Jerry here?"

"Out back, working on his bike."

I nodded. "Call me when it's done," I told them and watched them ride away. I headed around back and saw Jerry fiddling with his hog. He took a step back when he saw me.

"It's okay," I said. "Don't panic. I just want to talk."

"I've seen how you talk. Listen, I was just looking out for Colby."

"You were there to kill your girlfriend."

"She wasn't my girlfriend anymore. She was screwing everyone, including Kennedy, and finally —"

I held up my hand. "You don't say that, remember?" I moved closer. "Just like I don't say what I know about you." I met his gaze.

"Huh?"

"I know you've been around — all the way around."

He got it. "You can't prove that."

"Yeah, I probably can, but I don't want to. You know the rules are different here."

He nodded. "What do you want from me? I won't rat on Chase."

"What I want is for you to not go off on your own without informing the club. You can't make decisions like that without a vote. I don't want to find myself in the middle of a biker war because of you." I pointed at him. "You got it?"

He nodded. "Got it."

"Good." I smiled at him. "Now, what's wrong with your bike? Maybe I can help you."

He'd begun to tell me about the sound the bike made as it did over fifty miles an hour when Chase appeared. He looked at Jerry, moved his head toward the clubhouse, and Jerry hurried off.

"I want to talk to you," he said.

"So talk," I replied, glancing up from Jerry's bike.

"What's this shit about you being the negotiator with the TC?"

"I told you. You were drunk. Badger called me. They don't trust you. And to tell you the truth, neither do I."

"You ungrateful bastard," he said. "After all I've done for

you."

I stared at him. "Have you lost your mind? After all you've done for me? What in the fuck have you ever done for me?" I almost spit on the ground.

"I bailed you out. Drug dealers would have broken both your legs if I hadn't paid them off. And you'd be dead. You were nothing but a druggie loser who couldn't play football anymore. I paid twenty-two thousand dollars of your debt, plus dried out your druggie heart."

"Twenty-two thousand dollars?" I laughed. "And how much have I made you in the fights?"

"It's not the point. I saved your life."

"Once, and it cost you nothing. I've saved your hide so many times I can't count. I've taken a bullet for you. I've been stabbed and beaten for you. I've done all your fucking dirty work since day one. So, you know what, Chase? Fuck yourself!"

I suddenly noticed all the Banni standing around, just watching. Nuts came walking out in the middle of the yard. He stood between us. "We need to have church, now."

"We don't need church," Marcel called out. "We need a challenge. Some of us want a leadership change."

When in hell had he come back?

A few others shouted the same thing. Then I saw Colby. He walked into the group and stood beside Jerry. I was suddenly a little jealous. I knew they'd been lovers. He stayed silent though, and so did Jerry.

I didn't speak, just shook my head.

"You guys want church," Chase cried out. "Let's have it."

"Diego, you can take him," some of the guys were saying. "Do it. Take him. Put him down."

I walked inside. I didn't want to be leader, but somehow I knew that's where I was headed. I did everything anyway, without the badge.

An hour later, everyone who needed to be in attendance was. We were all crowded around the table in the back room. Only ten of us had seats. The rest stood quietly as Chase called the meeting to order.

"Some of you think that it's time for a leadership change. Rules say there has to be good reason to oust me unless someone physically challenges me." Chase looked at me. "You got reason to throw me out of this chair?"

I looked at Marcel, who was sitting on the edge of his seat, and gave him a murderous look. He sat back quietly. Then I looked at Chase. "No."

"Then it's over."

"Wait!" That was Johnny, one of the older members. He'd been with the Banni even before Chase. "I've been around a long time. And Chase, I'm sorry, but you're no leader. The Banni needs someone with heart—someone strong, determined, a guy we can respect and the other clubs fear." He looked right at me. "That guy is Diego. We all know it and so do you."

The noise began and didn't stop. The fists pounding on the table, the chanting of "challenge, challenge, challenge," didn't stop. Even those I thought loyal to Chase, like Nuts, were part of it. The only one who stayed quiet was Colby, and that's because he knew being leader was the last thing I wanted. But if the club voted that I was to challenge Chase, I'd have to unless he agreed to hand over the reins. And he'd never do that.

Chase was on his feet. He hollered out. "All in favor?"

That was it.

The room was deadly quiet all of a sudden.

Chase sneered at me. "I'm not going out easy." He ripped off his leader badge and tossed it onto the table, then walked out.

There were cheers, talking, and a lot of excitement while I

just sat there, stunned. Finally, I got up and walked out.

I went into the bike shop and stayed there, trying not to listen to the noise outside.

"You'll have to kill him. You know that, don't you? If you leave him alive, he'll stab you in the back first chance he gets."

I turned around to see Colby hugging the doorframe. I nodded. "I know that."

"It will a better club with you leading it."

"I never wanted this. I never wanted any of this." I didn't mean leadership; I meant all of it.

Colby came and stood beside me.

"I feel guilty and I shouldn't. I more than paid him back with my pain and my injuries. I've saved his life more than once. And yet, it was Chase who helped me to break the connection with drugs. I would have been a druggie on the street if not for him."

"And yet it wasn't unselfishness on his part, Diego." Colby met my gaze. "He saw your worth. He knew what you could give him. And you did. You didn't ask for this. The club did. If you don't want to kill him, then don't. But remember, Chase isn't going to take to being number two, even if you make him number two."

"Did you tell Jerry you loved him when he was fucking you?"

The question took Colby by surprise. "Where did that come from?"

"I don't know." I shrugged.

"I thought we were talking about Chase."

"We were. We are. I guess."

"And no," he said. "I've never told any man that except you." He reached out, and I pulled back. He nodded. "Okay. I understand. Sorry. I'm impulsive. I'm ... in love." He looked down. "I don't want you to be leader either. I know it's for the good of the club, but I'm afraid. I told you I lose everyone I love, and this is the first step."

"What? You think when I get to be leader someone is going to assassinate me?" I laughed.

Colby didn't return my laugh. "Just please, show no mercy," he said and walked off.

A few minutes later, I heard some loud voices. I went outside and found Colby arguing with his father. They stopped when they saw me.

Cledus came walking up to me as if his tail was on fire. "I should have been there."

"Where?"

"At church."

"You were notified. You didn't answer your phone."

"I object to this."

"Object to what, exactly?"

"To you leading the Banni. It's not right. It should be me or Jerry."

"Go ahead," I muttered, brushing past him. "You'd be doing me a favor."

Cledus reached out and grabbed my arm.

"Dad, don't," Colby cautioned.

I looked at his hand on my arm, then raised my head and looked directly at him. "I strongly recommend letting me go."

"And if I don't?" He squeezed harder.

"Then I'm going to knock you on your ass," I told him. "And it's going to hurt."

"You're too young to lead the Banni."

"You're not letting go." That was the last thing I said before I kneed him in the balls and had my hand on his throat. He was on the ground. I released him. "Don't do that," I said and kept walking.

I knew Colby had gone to help him up. It was his father.

What do you want? Probably he'd chew me out, but I didn't have a choice. That's all I was, someone who needed to keep proving himself over and over until one day someone came along and got the better of me. Everyone had his day. Mine hadn't come yet, but it would.

I went for my bike. I needed air and space. I needed to think. I rode until the sun went down, then stopped by my mother's to share a cup of coffee.

"What's bothering you, Diego," she asked.

"Nothing," I said, smiling at her.

"When you were a boy, you always got that look on your face when you were troubled."

I was never a boy. From the time my dad left, I had to be a man, had to grow up fast, look after things. I was worrying about paying the bills when I was eight.

"Diego, you talk to me now."

I stared at large television on mute and swallowed some more of my coffee. It was a football game. How fucking ironic.

"Diego." My mother raised her voice from where she rocked in her recliner. "Talk to me."

"My life is a mess, Mama." I stood. "There's nothing you can do about it."

"And you, what can you do about it?" she insisted.

I shook my head. "Nothing. I'm trapped like I've always been trapped. And now I guess my fate is sealed."

"Why?"

I saw her tremble, tears on her cheeks.

"I'm about to become the leader of the Banni." I met her gaze.

She lowered her head.

I walked into the kitchen, put the cup in the sink, and I heard her begin to sob as if her heart were breaking. I closed my eyes. I wished I could cry like that, but I'd forgotten how.

I stepped onto the porch and breathed the night air. The rain was coming. Seconds later, that little woman who'd given birth to me had me in an iron grip. She turned me to face her. "Please, don't."

I stroked her dark hair. "No choice. And, Mama, it's not just my life now, it's my heart. I think it's broken even worse than my life."

"Tammy?"

I shook my head. "Tammy would be easy. It's far worse than you could imagine."

She searched my face. "Colby," she said.

My eyes widened.

She placed fingers to my lips. "I'll never say it again."

I swallowed hard.

"You've always been a survivor, Diego, from the moment you took your first breath. Keep your love inside and never let them see it. They'll destroy you for it."

I nodded, biting my bottom lip.

She hugged me to her. "All the sacrifice you've done for me. I love you so much. If you have to challenge that bastard, kill him."

I smiled, and she released me. That's what Colby had told me to do. The two people I . . . yes, God . . . loved more than anything, had told me not to leave Chase alive.

When I returned to the clubhouse, everyone was drunk, including the bare-chested women, who were barely able to swing off the posts.

Marcel swaggered over with Jerry and sat down at a table with me. I didn't want to ask where Colby was.

Marcel brought me a beer, and I drank it, while, ironically, Marcel and Jerry seem to be flirting with each other. I knew Jerry could swing both ways, but Marcel surprised me.

"How many orgasms you think you can get in a night, Diego?" Marcel smirked at me.

"I'm not playing this game with you," I told him.

"Come on," Jerry coaxed. "Chicken or what? Tell us. I bet you could do three or four."

Colby walked into the room now. He looked relieved when he saw me. He came over and took a seat next to Jerry. "What's all this?" he asked.

Marcel elbowed him. "Questions and shit . . . truth time. Asked Diego about orgasms."

Colby grinned at me. "So? What's your answer, stud?"

"Not playing," I replied, looking away.

"All you got to say" — Jerry lifted his beer — "is one, two, or ten."

"Ten?" I looked at him.

Colby reached over and took a swig of my beer. "I'd guess three?" He looked at me.

I stood up.

"Poor sport," Jerry threw at me.

I walked outside, ignoring some girl's innuendo.

Colby joined me seconds later. "You all right?"

"Don't play with me," I snapped.

"I'm not . . . I mean . . ." He sighed. "I'm horny."

"Jesus." I swore and walked down the steps.

"Take me for a ride," he called out.

I stared at him.

"Okay, I'll ride with you. Let's go."

"Where are we going?" I asked him.

"I have something to tell you."

I followed him. "Fuck the bikes. Let's walk."

We walked a ways down the road without talking. That was nice.

"I heard Chase wants this challenge over with. He's talking Friday night."

I shrugged. "Whatever. Hope you weren't mad about what happened earlier — your dad and me."

He shook his head. "Dad thinks he should be leader. He's not up for it in any way. And my feelings for my dad are not about protection."

"Okay, I know what you mean by that. You said you weren't going to tell him you knew. Did you change your mind?"

"I'm torn. Sometimes I just want to let it all out, tell him I know, that I hate him for what he did. Anyway, it hasn't made me fonder of him. I'm waiting for the right time to really have it out with him after the police confirm everything. But if you kill Chase beforehand, that's fine, too. I feel so — "

I put my hands on his shoulders. "Tell me how it makes you feel."

"Why do you want to be burdened with all this? You've got enough to deal with."

"I want to know."

His expression softened. He stroked my cheek. I moved away in case someone saw him. "Colby, don't."

"I know. I can only touch you in my dreams."

I began to walk again. He fell in step beside me. All around us was nothing but trees, and I imagined pulling Colby into those woods and . . . I told myself . . . *control . . . control.*

"I feel so empty, like a part of me has been cut off. Garnet should be here, but she's gone. You know?"

I nodded.

"Now, it's my heart." He looked at me. "Damn you, Diego."

I looked up at the night sky.

He placed a hand on my back. "You hold it all in. Where do you put it?"

"I don't know."

"All your life, you've looked after everything and everyone. Sometimes I just want to look after you."

I glanced at him. "Don't worry about me."

"Does your mother know?"

I nodded. "She knows a lot more than she should."

"What do you mean?"

"She knows about you."

"How?"

I shook my head. "She knows me."

"She knows you're gay?"

"No. She knows my heart."

"Are you saying . . . something?" He met my gaze.

"Yeah." I nodded. "Something." I took his arm and pulled him into the trees and through a clearing.

He was laughing. "Where are we going?"

I was getting hit with tree branches and stumbling over my own feet, and then I saw it. A beautiful, big tree, standing all alone in the woods. I pressed Colby against the huge trunk.

He was breathing hard, his eyes sparkling like diamonds. "What are you doing?" he asked me.

"Making love to you," I told him, and he wound his arms around my neck, and we kissed, a tender kiss filled with passion and promise. I reared back, and he opened my shirt and pressed his lips to my chest. I held his head there for a moment, my eyes closed. "My Colby," I whispered.

I felt tears threaten. I pushed them back. I hadn't cried since I realized my career in the NFL had ended before it had even begun. No. No sentiment allowed, boys.

I turned him around and reached down to undo his pants. I pulled them down as our heavy breathing seemed to amplify around us in the still night. I fondled his hard cock and spread him open with my fingers, entering him fast. Against the tree I pumped frantically, looking for the release that only could be found in another man's arms. "Colby," I groaned as I came inside him, and Colby grasped the tree bark with both hands.

I pulled out of him and turned him around. He clung to me, his fingers bunched up in my vest. "Say it," he urged. "Just say it."

I lowered my head on his shoulder for a second until I could speak again, then I pulled away. "Don't make me," I pleaded. "I can't. Tell me to kill a man, I will. Tell me to face an army of enemy bikers, I'll be there. But damn it all, Colby, shit, don't ask me to say I love you because it's too much."

I pulled up my pants and buttoned my shirt. I watched as he did up his own pants, then brushed by me. "We better get back. It's starting to rain."

"Go on. I've got somewhere else to be."

"Where?" He looked at me.

"I'm going home to my place. I need serenity before the fight. Call me and let me know when it's going down. I'll be there."

He nodded, and I watched him disappear through the trees. I thought about fucking in the bushes when I was younger. Never thought I'd be doing it again at my age. Life was funny.

It was pouring by the time I got home. I wanted to open the windows. My small apartment above the club smelled musty. I was rarely there. I wondered if I should give up the place and just move all my shit into the clubhouse.

I sprayed some air freshener, then regretted it. The place smelled like a brothel after that. I stripped off my clothes, took a shower, and fell into bed. I slept for twelve hours.

When I finally did get up, it was Thursday afternoon. I was making coffee when someone rang my doorbell. I dashed to the window to see a slew of bikes downstairs.

There were a few soldiers wearing the colors of the Texas Crushers. Shit. That's all I needed. I took a pistol out of the drawer and loaded it. I was ready.

I went to the door. "Who is it?"

"Badger. I come in peace, man."

"Really, 'cause I got a pistol here that's ripe for firing."

"Can we talk?"

I hesitated, then opened the door, jumping back, gun raised. "What do you want?"

"You can pat me down, man. I'm clean."

"Turn around."

I felt him all over. Satisfied, I put the gun in my pants. "Talk."

"I heard you're challenging Chase for leadership."

"Club decision."

"Good decision."

"Okay, so you've come to sign up for my fan club?"

"Hardly. I just need to know who I'm dealing with from now on. I'd love to see that fight."

"It's sold out," I said with a sneer.

"You wouldn't consider switching sides?"

"You offering me a grunt job in your club, Badger?" I lifted an eyebrow.

"I'm offering you the VP position."

I was stunned. "You have a VP."

"Not your worry. You interested?"

Damn. This would solve all my problems with Colby. We wouldn't see each other. That would be a good thing. But I couldn't. I was Banni. You didn't just switch teams.

"Sorry, no can do," I said.

"I want you, Diego. One day, you'll be with me, at my side. We'd be good friends, you and I. We're both smart and unbeatable."

"Thanks for the sentiment. I'm hoping if I become leader,

we can have good relations. Together, we could own this state. There's plenty to go around."

"I agree. I like the way you think." He slapped me on the back. "Let me know when it's over, and you are where you should have been all along. We'll talk. We can strike a good deal, man—something good for both clubs."

"Okay." I nodded. "I'll be in touch."

"Oh, and as a goodwill gesture, I have some info for you."

I waited.

"I found out from someone outside the club that Kennedy was a poofter. Seems that Colby guy you've taken under your wing has tendencies. Outsiders say he's frequented the baths before. Watch yourself in the middle of the night."

A lump settled in my throat. "I'll keep my eye on him."

He nodded. I watched him leave and closed the door behind him. To say I was scared was an understatement. If Colby had been seen at gay spots, God only knows if anyone would have seen me and reported it to someone.

I went out for some fried shrimp and chips and came back with a bottle of whiskey. I drank myself to sleep in front of the television while the rain kept on pouring down outside.

Nuts called me Friday afternoon to tell me the fight was at midnight at the scrapyard. Nuts hadn't said much about the challenge of Chase's leadership. I wasn't sure how he felt about it. "Hey," I said before he hung up. "Who's your money on?" It was meant to be a joke, but then I realized the guys were probably already putting money down.

"My money's on you, man," he said.

"I know you and Chase are . . ."

"I go with the winner. See you tonight." He hung up.


The rain had stopped, but the wind was coming off the water strong tonight. I was half frozen by the time I got to the scrapyard. All the bikes were lined up out front of the office. It looked like everyone was here.

"Where's Chase?" I asked Nuts, who had parked beside me.

"In the office, composing himself. I told him to surrender."

"Why? He has a right to defend his leadership."

"You're going to kill him, Diego." Nuts met my eyes. "I don't want to see Chase die. You're the better leader, but he's still my friend."

"I won't kill him unless I have to." As I said it, I knew it was true.

"But you have to." He spit out a shell. "We all know it. So does he. The honorable thing is for him to fight you and lose, then coward out and live."

Colby pulled up now with Jerry behind him. Those two were like clones. I didn't like being jealous, but somehow, seeing those two together got to me.

They both nodded to me and walked by. I sighed. I wanted to get this over with.

As if reading my mind, Nuts said, "It's time. I'll get Chase."

A few minutes later, the men were gathered around. I stood in the center, waiting. Then Nuts came out with Chase.

Chase looked at me.

I nodded.

"I should have let you die," he muttered.

"I don't want to do this," I shook my head. "You leave me no choice."

"You think I'm just going to hand this over to you?" He held up the badge. "You're going to bleed for it."

Nuts put up his hands. "No weapons allowed. This is a fair fight. Last man standing is the leader of the Banni." He moved aside.

It would have been easy, except in my heart, I still had gratitude for Chase for drying me out and saving me from the dealers, even if I did pay him back a hundredfold. Chase had given me something to believe in, a family, a new reason to get up in the morning, even if it wasn't the most honorable one in the world.

So when I could have put him down, I didn't. I took his beating for longer than I had to, at least allowing him to look good, until finally I couldn't anymore. I landed him a couple of good hits, and he was out. When I put him down, he wasn't getting back up, but I hadn't killed him. In spite of all the good advice, and in spite of the fact that I knew it had been a mistake—one that would come back and bite me in the ass—I let him live.

Beaten and battered, the men crowded around while Nuts went to tend to Chase. "Take him to the hospital," I called out. Several of the Banni scrambled to do my bidding.

At one point, I met Colby's gaze. I knew what he was telling me. There was fear and disappointment in that gaze. I looked away, and the boys lifted me up and carried me into the clubhouse.

Tammy was already sewing the patch on my jacket as pitchers of beer were being shoved at me and poured on me.

Tammy came to sit on my knee, holding my jacket.

The boys were chanting to her to take off her top and, before I knew it, my face was being pushed in between her bare breasts.

More booze and more girls sitting on me, it was one big party. I was getting so drunk I didn't know what the hell was going on. Naked girls danced in front of me and my head spun.

I finally managed to get to my feet and stagger to the toilet. When I turned around again, Colby was there. He'd closed us in. "Hey," I said. His face blurred in front of me.

"Come to congratulate me?"

"You can hardly stand up."

"Oops, come to lecture me." I laughed and reached out for the sink.

"Why didn't you kill him, Diego?"

"You're a bloodthirsty one." I laughed again.

"He's got friends in the club. Are you making him VP?"

"Colby, fuck, I don't know. Leave me alone, okay? I can't . . . I'm drunk. It's feels good, so go away." I tried to push past, but he didn't move. "Colby, come on."

A second later, he let me go.

Tammy grabbed my hand in the hallway. "Dance with me," she said.

"Oh no, Tammy," I groaned. But she was in my arms and swaying with me to some song I'd never heard before. I was about to collapse.

"I'm going to be your old lady, right?" She looked up at me.

I shook my head. I was about to say something else when I saw a flash of lights. "Get down!" I yelled.

I hit the floor, Tammy with me. Bullets from automatic rifles shattered the windows. "Colby," I murmured. I looked at Tammy. "Stay down." I crawled across the floor.

I saw two men dead. I careened around the corner to see Colby in the corner. He wasn't moving. "Colby?" I got up and ran to him.

When he turned his head to look up at me, he winced.

"Oh, thank God." I fell on my knees beside him. "Are you all right?"

He nodded. "Got knocked over when he went down." He pointed to the body beside him. It was Dave—or what was left of him.

"Who did it?" he asked.

"Someone who wants a share of the drug trade, someone

connected to Teresa that we didn't know about. Maybe she had family."

We got to our feet.

"One with automatic weapons," Colby said, glancing at Jerry.

"I didn't say they were the Brady Bunch."

I walked out in the hall to see what the damage was. The two dead were Jackson and Giles, two guys who'd been with Chase long before me. Everyone else was fine. It looked like we'd be having a funeral. Then once I found out who was responsible, it was payback time.

As I stood there, Tammy came to hug onto me. The men were all looking at me, even Colby. It was official. I was now the leader of the Banni.

# CHAPTER SEVEN

Colby

I fell asleep in the upstairs bedroom Cherise had assigned me and awoke early in the morning to the tune of Eva Cassidy singing 'Autumn Leaves' on somebody's radio. I held my breath and listened. The music was coming from outside. Shit. My head felt like I'd gone twelve rounds with Mike Tyson. Mad hangover. I went to the bathroom, thought I'd puke, but didn't. I washed my face with cold water and soap, then opened the medicine cabinet. Relieved when I found a bottle of aspirin, I opened it—after a lot of wrestling and cursing under my breath. Why did Cherise feel the need for childproof caps in a house full of bikers?

*Oh. Wait. I forgot.* My sister and the kids were here.

The full horror of everything that had passed these last few days hit me then. I swallowed four aspirin with a handful of water and examined my face in the mirror. I looked like hell. I rarely drank, and I sure as hell had never buried a body before. Getting rid of Teresa was a lot harder than it looked on TV and in the movies. It had been horrible.

I went downstairs, happily detected coffee in the kitchen, and poured myself a cup from the carafe.

Eva Cassidy's haunting voice went on about how when autumn leaves fell, that's when she missed her man. I knew it was the doomed songstress because I'd listened to her obsessively when I first discovered her. Now she was gone, lost to cancer too young. I gazed out the window at the wal-

114

nut trees, jostling for space in Cherise's backyard. I felt Eva was trying to tell me something.

*She's with me. Garnet's with me! We are everywhere. We are here, high in the sky. She is the jewel of the clouds.*

Something in me broke. Sometimes, I don't think I can live without her, and yet, every day I do. Sometimes the pain is unbearable. Those are the days I imagine her locked up as some deviant's sex slave. I have the rare good day when I can almost pretend she's gone off to a wonderful life as a wife and mom, but I know better. I don't know when I stopped hearing her voice in my soul, but I just don't feel her anymore.

I wanted to cry.

Instead, I swallowed the coffee as fast as I could, hoping it would ease the dull ache behind my eyes.

And in my bones.

How does God, if there is one, help people endure excruciating loss? Somehow, we keep moving. The worst thing imaginable happens to us, but we keep living. Suddenly, I resented more than ever that my sister had named her baby Garnet. She had no right to do that when she let our wonderful girl be abused. She could have done more.

*Enough. Stop it. She was a kid.* Another thought came to me. She was scared. It must have been horrendous living like that.

My only consolation as I fought for my equilibrium is that I do believe in God for people like Garnet. And I believe she is in Heaven.

"Look after her, Eva," I whispered up to the sun. "Hold her close. Please don't let her fall."

The tears started to come again, but I fought them off, topping up my cup. Thankful that Eva had stopped singing, I went outside to find Cherise sitting on the top step right outside the door.

She looked up at me, smiling.

I smiled back, noticing the old radio at her feet and the bowl of shelled peas in her lap. I knelt, removing the bowl of unshelled peas beside her. I kept my gaze averted because I was certain she could see right through me. I broke open a thick and hearty-looking pod and let the peas slide into my hand. The spent shell went into a bowl beside the radio and the peas into the one on Cherise's lap.

She leaned against me in an endearing way. "My Diego used to do this with me when he was a kid. He loved eating peas right out of the pod." She leaned away again, and I tried to block the memory of doing this with Ma before she went crazy. Before I hated her.

Cherise could have been out of another time and place, and yet, here she was. I was so glad some things didn't change. People still shelled peas and listened to the radio.

"Everybody loves peas out of the pod," I said, though I worried too much time had passed since she'd made her comment.

She turned to look at me. "You're worried about something, Colby."

I was so surprised I didn't know what to say. I dickered around in my fuzzy head, trying to think of some sort of response when I heard the roar of a bike. We both turned to look, and there was Detective Duchesne coming up her driveway. He looked damned scared of his Harley if you ask me.

He had trouble turning the damned thing off and almost hit a tree.

"Howdy," he said, dismounting. The bike fell to the ground. If any of the other guys had seen him let that chopper fall, they'd have freaked. Me, I knew Pa had given it to him. I wanted the bike to die.

"Howdy," I said back, watching him stand the bike back up again. I was pleased to see him.

"You want privacy?" Cherise asked, looking uneasy.

"Naw." I shook my head. I had no idea if she knew, and I didn't care if Diego had told her about Garnet Beauty. "Cherise, please meet Detective Rogan Duchesne."

"We've met before, but mighty nice to see you again, Miz Champagne." He shook her hand, and her cheeks flamed.

He glanced at me, an odd expression on his face. "I have some news. Sorta."

"About my sister?"

He nodded.

I became aware of Cherise's hard stare. I swallowed hard. I wanted news, but could I take whatever he had to tell me?

"Good or bad?" I asked.

He scratched him chin. "Knowing you, it's bad news. But there's some good. I'll start with the news that the state of Georgia exhumed the body of their Jane Doe."

I split open another pea. "And?"

He grimaced. "It wasn't Garnet Beauty."

Cherise turned to look at me again.

"They're sure?" Man, I felt crushed.

"Turns out their Jane Doe had a cleft palate, and she was pregnant at the time of death. She wasn't a little kid. She was a small woman. They're thinking maybe Mexican. Don't know how they let that one slip through their hands like that. We did them a favor. Now they can launch a fresh investigation."

"What about Alabama?"

"Now that we know Garnet wasn't the Jane Doe from Georgia, I have to go through the channels again to order an exhumation in Alabama." He put his hands on his hips and dropped them again.

The peas grew warm in my hand. I was afraid I'd crush them into soup, so I let them fall into Cherise's bowl.

"I have other news," he said, watching my face carefully.

"Colby, I know this is damned hard for you to hear, but we interviewed Cledus after you gave me the information from June. We hauled his ass in. He lied a bunch at first, claiming he had no idea your sister was being kept in a cage. Then he admitted June had told him. He claims he confronted your mother, who then told him she no longer kept her there.

"When you called him and told him Garnet was missing, it was as big a surprise to him as it was to you."

"And you believe him?"

He nodded, slowly, a look of puzzlement on his face. "We gave Cledus a lie detector test. He passed. So I don't believe he had any knowledge of the crime against Garnet."

The beautiful voices of the Wilson Phillips trio were on the radio singing 'Hold On.' How apt. I had to hold on—for my sister's sake. I had to wait and keep hoping. Damn. I'd been so sure my father had killed her.

I couldn't help it. A couple of tears fell. Rogan Duchesne reached down and grabbed my neck in a comforting gesture.

Cherise put down her bowl and put her arms around me. I listened to the song and its advice to hold on for one more day. Cherise and I sat there for the longest time.

I was aware of Duchesne leaving us, heard the roar of the chopper again. But I was too torn with grief to break away from Diego's mother. It was the closest I'd ever be likely to be near him again.

I was stunned when Duchesne roared back. He dismounted, kicked the stand, and the bike stayed where it was, engine running.

"Colby, I have an idea. Why not go visit your ma?"

"Visit her? I want to kill her."

Cherise's hold on me tightened.

"I talked to her, and she's plumb crazy—"

"You talked to her?"

"Best I could. Maybe she'll open up to you. Maybe you

can break through the veil between reality and madness."

"No. I can't."

"I'll go with you," Cherise said. She lifted her face from my shoulder and looked at me, a defiant gleam in her eye. "I need to know what sort of mother keeps her baby in a cage."

"Cool," Duchesne said and raced back to his bike, as though it were a done deal.

Fuck. I did not want to see my mother again, unless it was at her funeral.

"It's okay to have a crazy mama," Cherise said.

"If you say so." I shifted out of her embrace. God. Would the indignities never end? My mother had abandoned me, and now I had to go visit her?

"Every Southern family has bat-shit-crazy people, honey. Like my favorite character on *Designing Women* once observed, "Nobody asks you in the South if you have crazy people in your family. They just ask which side they're on."

I couldn't help laughing. She was okay, Cherise. "Which side are yours on?"

"Both." She joined in my laughter.

"Me, too." I sobered up quickly. I had no idea which loony bin my mother was in. I didn't want to ask my dad or my sister. Calvin would know, but he'd blab to my dad. I went back into the house and grabbed my cell phone. I switched it on, about to call Detective Duchesne, but he'd beaten me to the punch. He'd sent a text message with the name of the facility, phone number, and visiting hours of seven-thirty to eight-thirty in the evening.

I couldn't deal with this right now. Then I looked at the property on the other side of the road, kitty-corner to Cherise's, where the clubhouse and scrapyard were located. The mortuary hearse had arrived to collect the bodies of Dave and the other two dead Banni members, and I knew I had to deal. I'd never forgive myself if Evangeline died without my attempt to communicate with her at least once.

A shower first, I decided. Then more coffee. And then I would call the hospital. It was in New Orleans, which surprised me. Evangeline had always hated the Big Easy. But she was nuts and had probably no idea where the hell she was.

Back upstairs, I rifled through my belongings. Somebody had washed and dried my discarded clothing. Cherise? My sister? A house elf? I picked up clean underwear, socks, a T-shirt, and jeans, and dumped the dirt-stained stuff I'd been wearing on the floor.

Checking up and down the hallway that nobody was around, I darted naked across to the bathroom. I was about to close the door when a voice said, "Not so fast, laddie."

Laddie. It could only be Sue Ellen. I walked in, picked off a towel from a stack on a wall shelf, and covered up my twig and giggleberries.

"Relax, Colby. I've seen it all before," Sue Ellen grumped.

"What's wrong?" I asked. Was she mad I hadn't bumped off Teresa myself? Bumped off. Sheesh. Remembering the woman's burial gave me the creeps.

"You're going to visit your ma without me? And with her?" She jerked her thumb toward Cherise, who'd showed up beside her.

"Sorry, Colby," Jerry said, looking at me between the two women's shoulders.

"Can't a guy get any privacy around here?" I backed away from the door, and the towel fell to the ground. Oops. I picked it up again and held it to me, all I had between me and two feudin' women.

"What's going on?" Marcel asked, his head bobbing over the others.

"Oh, great," I muttered. "Anyone else wanna see me naked?"

A fifth head loomed over Sue Ellen's shoulder.

Dang. It was Diego. Oh, no. Now I was gonna get a hard-on. That would be embarrassing.

He wiggled his eyebrows up and down then vanished. I would have laughed, except that I really did want to be alone.

"I'm taking a shower," I said with as much dignity as a nekkid man could. "We'll discuss it the moment I'm dressed."

I closed the door on the huffy-looking women and a grinning Jerry.

Fifteen minutes later I was feeling much better. A fresh cup of coffee and wonderful smells of what suspiciously looked like a pan of my sister's signature beignets, I found I had a much better outlook on life.

"Cavendish Hospital called your cell phone. I took the liberty of taking the call," Sue Ellen said. "Apparently Detective Duchesne informed them that you want to see your mother. We're scheduled to visit Evangeline at one o'clock."

"One o'clock? But I thought visiting hours were at night."

"They said she does better during the day, and since you've never visited her before, they want you to see her at her best." Sue Ellen slid a glance toward Cherise. "I told them I'm your aunt, and we're accompanying you. I understand you would like us both there. I haven't mentioned it to June Gold. Should I?"

"No," I responded around a mouthful of warm, crispy fried goodness. In spite of everything, June hadn't lost her touch. "I'll talk to her. Where is she?"

Cherise and Sue Ellen exchanged glances. "She and Judd are moving out today. They're taking the kids." Sue Ellen looked upset. "They don't like the club stuff that's going on." She dropped her voice. "Three deaths last night, Colby.

Lucky we have a mortician in the family. It ain't easy explaining three deaths to the authorities, you know. The kids heard the shooting, but Judd managed to convince them it was fireworks."

I winced, eyeing the pan of beignets that had my name all over them, and sighed. "Where is she?" I asked again.

Sue Ellen pointed over her shoulder to the backyard. I went outside and found my sister and Judd on their knees, folding fresh-dried laundry from a hamper, packing it into suitcases. The kids were playing football with Marcel, Garnet shrieking with laughter. She hated dolls. She was a tomboy through and through.

My sister leaned back on her haunches, scraped a stray tendril of hair from her eyes with the back of her hand and glared at me. "We need to talk, Colby."

"Sure thing." I think.

Little Garnet saw me and ran over, thrusting her arms up high. Her sweet face tasted of powdered sugar and choux pastry. She tucked her head under my chin as I rained kisses on her forehead.

"Don't wanna go," she said into my neck.

"I don't want you to either, sweetie." I dropped more kisses on her face, making her laugh.

"Get down, Garnet. Go play with Henry. Mama and Uncle Colby got bizzness to discuss." Her sharp tone seemed to frighten my niece. Henry, Garnet's three-year-old brother, looked scared of his mom. Wow. I hoped this apple, er . . . peach, had fallen far from our maternal tree. If I ever had any inkling that June laid a hand on either of the children, I'd string her up alive.

I followed her into the house where the others were demolishing the beignets.

She made a tsking sound, walking from room to room until she found one that was unoccupied. As soon as we were alone, she turned on me.

"I found a new space in New Orleans. I want you to come and look at it. I'm supposed to be getting a hefty insurance check." She gave me a look I couldn't quite identify.

"Well, that's good."

"Yeah. It's right next door to the old space. It's that weird candle shop that was the bane of my existence."

I hadn't thought it was a weird place. The woman had been a naturopath who sold old-fashioned drafts and tonics, as well as herbal teas and infused candles. She'd always been nice to me.

"She selling out?" I asked, dreading the answer.

"No. She died of smoke inhalation from the fire."

I was really sorry to hear she'd died.

My sister gave me a significant look. "I'd like you to come take a look at it this afternoon and make an offer to her family."

I wanted to make sure I'd heard her right. "You want me to buy it for you? You don't want to use any of the insurance money?"

"This happened to me because of you," she snapped, her voice rising. "I need every dime of—" Her head swiveled toward the door. "Garnet Beauty, get the hell away from here! Git outside, unless you want a spanking!"

My four-year-old niece's face crumpled, and she ran off crying.

"Was that necessary?" I asked June.

"You judging me, Colby?" She narrowed her eyes at me.

"Our sister lived through horrific abuse." I kept my voice low. "Just know that I'm gonna be watching you, June Gold. Like a hawk."

She glared at me, then seemed to soften. She wanted the money. Pure and simple.

"I've never hit them. Until I lost my bakery, I never yelled at 'em once." She bit her lip. "I'm in a bad mood all the time now."

"What time do you want me there today?"

"Four o'clock?" She wasn't telling; she was asking. I sensed she was tuning into Garnet, who was outside crying hysterically.

"I'll be there."

She hardly heard me. She fled from the room and headed back outside. I followed her, keeping my distance. I watched her take her daughter out of Judd's arms. She held the weeping little girl and comforted her.

I tried not to think about her calming our beaten, battered sister, and vowed to keep a close eye on my niece and nephew. I didn't care what she'd said. I didn't trust June. I hated to admit it, but it was how I felt.

"Everything okay?" Sue Ellen asked, coming to stand beside me.

"Sure." I sighed. I was doing a lot of that these days.

"How'd she take it?"

"I haven't told her yet. I have to meet her in New Orleans at four. She wants to take over the place next door to her bakery. I'm gonna try and buy it for her."

Sue Ellen put her hand to my cheek and gave me a tender smile. "You've always been so good to her."

I smiled back, flicking a glance at my sister, who was laughing now with her daughter. The sun came out so easily for Garnet.

It never had for the other one.

I thought the two moms, Jerry, and I would drive by car to New Orleans, but both women seemed offended at the suggestion.

"Get me on the back of that chopper," Cherise said to me.

Okey dokey, Smokey.

Jerry took his mom and Cherise rode with me. I was so

glad for the bike ride. In spite of my apprehension about visiting my mother, I felt the familiar tug of freedom riding always gives me. I wished Diego was with me, then pushed the thought from my mind.

The wind whipped my face, making me grin from my very soul the entire hour and ten minutes it took us to reach New Orleans.

It was great to be back where the action was. We slowed down some, cruising past the hordes of tourists in the French Quarter and its crazy mecca, Bourbon Street. Many were drunk, even at this hour. Talk about a boulevard of broken dreams.

We passed them, and I turned on St Ann Street. I smiled when I spotted Cafe Lafitte In Exile, the city's oldest gay bar. I turned on Burgundy, still part of the old quarter, and saw the building looming ahead on the left.

I felt instantly uneasy the moment we saw Cavendish House. It was one of those big, fancy homes with wrought-iron gates that were typical of the city in the nineteenth-century. Having never been inside a mental asylum before, I listened for groans and shrieks as we got off the bikes and approached the entrance, but all was quiet. We walked up the stairs, and for one split second, I wanted to run. The place felt oppressive and stifling, in spite of its neat appearance and proliferation of flowers out front.

Sue Ellen must have sensed my apprehension because she caught my hand in hers and I held tight. I braced myself for the moment I saw my mother. I tried to remember any happy feelings I had for her. There were none. I do remember the last time I'd seen her. I was young—just five years old. June was four, Garnet two. It had been the day Ma announced she was leaving me and Pa.

"I don't want him," she'd whispered across the kitchen table, as though I was deaf and couldn't hear her. "I don't want any man."

She'd planned it; I remember that clearly. She'd packed the night before, and anything she hadn't packed, two men in a truck soon removed from the premises. My father argued over her taking all our kitchen stuff and the TV.

"The boy and I need to live!" he'd implored her.

"No, you don't." She'd looked right at me when she said it. A cold, dead eye was the last thing I saw of her.

Oh, wait. That wasn't the last time I'd seen her. When I was twelve, I ran away from home and went to the Florida parishes to see my sisters. My ma was in bed. June opened the door. And that's when I discovered Garnet was gone. By the time I called Pa to alert him, and after he'd beaten me for running away, and the police came to interview Ma, she came out of her room. She was dressed in a flimsy, dirty robe and acted resentful about being dragged from her bed.

She gave me that same cold-fish look. I knew I was dead to her, and she hated me. I had no idea why. She was mean to the cops and said they were pigs.

"Christ, Evangeline," my father had said, wiping a hand across his mouth. "Answer their questions. How long has Garnet been missing?"

She went mad, chucking stuff, and got herself arrested. I didn't see her after that. I just had no desire to have her in my life. She has never made a lick of sense when I've spoken to her on the phone. The last time was twenty years ago. She called to report that it was hot on Saturn.

Yep. That news was sure worth a phone call.

In spite of the genteel appearance of the building, it was still a nut house. Our IDs were examined the moment a security guard opened the front door. He let us in, and I was intrigued to see the interior looked like a hospital clinic—one with a ton of security measures in force.

We each had to hand over every single personal item. We

had to entrust them to people we'd never met. Sue Ellen was okay about everything except her comb.

"A woman always needs to keep up a good appearance," she told the guard.

Apparently, the guard disagreed.

"It stays in the purse," he muttered.

We filled out forms, and the strange, antiseptic smell of the place hit me, leaving an unpleasant tingle at the back of my throat.

Jerry looked spooked as we went through one set of doors and our papers were scrutinized. A different guard pressed a buzzer in this long, narrow hallway and another door opened to a section that looked more like an office. Every desk was filled. We stood, huddled in a small, frightened group as a woman looked up from her seat and gestured toward us. She, too, examined our papers without a word.

There wasn't a single personal thing on any desk that I could see.

Perhaps they were all afraid of the implication that anything from their real lives might make them look . . . nuts.

She got up, took us past a maze of desks to another door. She pressed a buzzer, and a guard appeared. He, too, examined our papers. He led us to another door and pressed yet another button. We tipped out into the actual hospital ward, where another guard approached us.

"Which one of you is Colby Young?" he asked, gazing from me to Jerry.

"Me." I held up a hand.

"Dr. Warner would like to speak to you alone. The others can wait in the visiting room.

"Oh, but—" Sue Ellen began.

"Alone," the guard repeated.

I wasn't thrilled. Why did I need to see the doctor? I followed him to an office that looked as though somebody had tried hard to make order out of numerous files and stacks of books.

"Take a seat," the guard said. He stood behind me as I sat at the desk, wondering about the doctor who would be sitting in the big swivel chair opposite.

We both waited. I glanced over my shoulder. The guard was still there, staring at me as though I might go through files on the desk. If I'd been alone, I would have.

A door on the other side of the office opened and a middle-aged guy, who needed to lay off the cheesecakes, approached us.

"Colby?" he asked, a pleasant smile on his face.

"That's me." I shook his extended hand, not liking the cold, clammy feel to his palm.

We took our seats, and he gave me an appraising look.

"So, you're Colby."

I nodded.

"You're not what I imagined."

"What did you imagine?"

"Somebody more . . . unruly looking."

"Thank God I took a shower this morning," I said. That made him laugh.

"You have her sense of humor."

"She has a sense of humor?" Boy, did that surprise me. I couldn't remember seeing her laugh much unless it was the strange, maniacal cackle that would erupt for no apparent reason.

He gave me an appraising glance. "You're angry with her."

"Very. I'm here for one reason. I'm hoping she might finally tell me what she did to my sister." My voice broke. I took a deep breath.

A pained expression crossed his features.

"Andy, we'll be okay," he told the guard. "You can leave

us now. I'll call you in a few minutes."

The guard said nothing but left the room. I didn't get the feeling he was thrilled about leaving me alone with the doc.

"Colby, how much do you know about your mother's condition?"

"I know she's crazy."

His eyes hardened. "She's mentally ill."

"Same thing." What was I doing arguing with a mental health professional? All my life I'd feared winding up like Evangeline. My biggest fear has always been being subjected to electroshock therapy.

He shook his head. "Colby, I understand from your father and Detective Duchesne about recent events that have come to light. Before you talk to Evangeline, there are some things you need to know that may help you see her in a different way."

I said nothing. I highly doubted anything he told me would make me feel sorry for her.

"She's suffering from a severe case of puerperal psychosis."

I stared him. "Isn't that postpartum psychosis?"

He nodded. "Very good."

"But she's in her fifties and hasn't had a baby recently. Has she?"

He gazed down at his desk a moment. "You might be aware that Louisiana wasn't exactly a pioneer in the treatment of mental health when your mother became sick."

I had no idea. "Haven't given it much thought." I was getting restless now.

"When she became ill, puerperal psychosis wasn't even on the radar in terms of treatment. Women were treated as though the psychosis had nothing to do with childbearing. I'd say from the moment she had you, then June so close behind you, that she was in the middle of a psychotic break."

"Oh, so now it's my fault?"

"I didn't mean to imply that. She should never have had a third child."

"Apparently, she thought so, too," I said, bitterness dripping from my voice.

He leaned forward. "Colby, I know about the cage. I know what you've learned. But I want you to understand, she didn't keep Garnet in there as a punishment. She kept her in there to protect her." He paused. "She kept her in that cage so that she couldn't harm her own child."

# CHAPTER EIGHT

I didn't know what to say. I'd never heard such bullshit in my life.

"Women suffering from puerperal psychosis often see their baby dead. They have terrible dreams of blood and violence. When your mother became ill, the doctors treating her tried experimental drugs. They tried electroconvulsive therapy. That seemed to work for a time. It's a useful therapeutic tool in small doses. Evangeline had way too much, and it's erased portions of her memory. She has a baby doll she thinks is Garnet, and she becomes quite hysterical if anyone tries to take it from her."

*Sheesh.*

"Thoughts?" he asked me.

I almost spat on his office floor. "She abused Garnet Beauty. I don't care what she told you. I believe June Gold when she tells me that Evangeline beat up our sister and kept her caged because she hated her."

He looked stunned. "That doesn't sound like the Evangeline I know."

"Oh, boy." I shook my head. "You've fallen for her, too."

"That's insulting."

"No, it's not. Men have fallen for her since she was the Stonewall Peach Queen. Go ahead and tell me she's never mentioned that fact."

His cheeks flushed. "Once or twice."

"Crazy or not, she still knows how to manipulate a man."

He seemed thrown by my statement. He took a moment

to compose himself. "I'm going to ask you to go easy on her. She has good days and bad. Today is . . . a bad one. She's worried about her baby. She's on a good regime of psychotropic medications, but one of our new nurses didn't watch her closely enough yesterday, and Evangeline didn't swallow her pills. She's taken them today, though."

"And you think it's okay for me to see her on a bad day?" I was incredulous.

"A bad day for her is where she's morose, acts sad about every little thing going on around her. I should tell you she has no memory of anything that happened to Garnet. She thinks she's very much alive. I wanted to explain this to you before you saw her." He paused. "I want you to have a few moments alone with her before your companions join you."

I wasn't sure I wanted to be alone with her. "She hates me," I blurted.

"No, she doesn't, Colby."

"She does. Always did. She abandoned me."

"No. She became sick."

"She. Abandoned. Me. Walked out and left me with my abusive father. I had a revolting childhood with and without her, but not as bad as Garnet."

I almost said I'd lost interest in seeing her now but held my tongue.

"It was her sickness. She blamed your father for getting her pregnant. You're just an extension of him."

I could see that. I said nothing more. I was hating every second of this.

"I'll take you to see her," he said. "I'll stay with you, in case she becomes agitated."

We left his office and walked down several narrow corridors that felt like they might close in on me. I struggled to breathe at one point and realized they'd done something funny to the air.

"What's going on?" I asked. I seemed suddenly high, light-headed.

And then we walked into a visiting room, and there was Evangeline by the window, standing, skinny as ever, her blonde hair not as shiny as it once was. As I faced her, I was shocked to see how sparse her hair was, as though she had ripped patches from her head. Her skin was kind of gray, but she giggled.

It was whatever they had pumped into their air ducts. It was slight, almost undetectable, but I had an allergy to nitrous oxide, otherwise known as laughing gas. It made me feel breathless and panicky, the opposite effect it was supposed to have.

My lungs ached as I fought for air.

She held the baby doll in her arms, and to my left I saw Cherise, Jerry, and Sue Ellen, watching through a window. Jerry looked stricken.

"Hi," I said, focusing on Evangeline, who looked unaware of her audience.

"Hi," she said, rocking the baby back and forth. "Oh. A dirty diaper." She flung herself on a chair, humming some strange tune that hurt my ears.

"Is that your baby?" I asked, taking a seat opposite her. The doctor moved silently near me, taking another seat. She didn't seem to notice him, either.

She stopped undressing the doll and gave me a curious look. She gazed at me, taking stock of me. She said nothing, sucking her bottom lip as she finished undressing the doll. It wore a baby diaper folded many times over.

"Is that Garnet?" I asked, aware of Doctor Warner stiffening beside me.

Her gaze came up to meet mine, and her blue eyes turned deadly.

"No. It's Colby." She got a vicious look on her face and

began spanking the doll so hard it flew off her lap and hit the table near her.

She began to laugh. "Bad, Colby. Bad."

I got up. I'd had enough. "Still think she doesn't hate me?" I asked the stunned-looking doctor and walked out of the room.

"That was intense," Jerry said, once we went through the whole security rigmarole and got back outside. I hated the looks of sympathy on all their faces. I didn't want sympathy. I'd gotten it all my life. Jerry's family had been the only ones not to see me as a charity case, as the kid who needed a warm meal. They'd genuinely loved me.

"I'm riding with you," Sue Ellen said, clearly struggling with her emotions. "Let's go have lunch at Willie Mae's."

I didn't argue, though I didn't think I'd be able to eat. The wind bitch-slapping me cured me of my creepy visit to the bughouse. By the time we'd made our way back to New Orleans' Seventh Ward and Willie Mae's Scotch House on St Ann Street, I was famished. We parked the choppers and walked inside the white clapboard building.

This neighborhood has a bad reputation with some folk. I have no idea why. When Hurricane Katrina hit the city, I was impressed with how many volunteers showed up to help old Willie Mae and her kin fix up the badly damaged restaurant.

Jerry and I inhaled the scent of the best fried chicken in town. Cherise and Sue Ellen were having a blast, chatting away with the waiter and comparing red bean recipes. I don't care what they mutually decided, the Scotch House made the best red beans in the city, second to none.

We ordered our food, and the women regaled us with amusing anecdotes about New Orleans back in the day. It must have been something in the fifties, that's for sure.

"We want to go to the beauty parlor," Sue Ellen suddenly announced, as I picked up the check. "We'll see you over at the bakery."

"Or what's left of it," I said.

We had a little over an hour before I was supposed to meet June. As the women hurried off down the street, Jerry and I rode our bikes over to my pool hall. I'd been in touch with my guys who'd been managing it. Just like my dad, I kept my business and gang life separate. I'd stayed in touch with Don Ritchie, the manager, and he looked wiped out.

"'Bout time you showed up," he said. "We got a lot of deposits we haven't made and bills to be paid." He shoved some moneybags at me, and a slew of final notices. I just about went bonkers. I couldn't say anything though. I hadn't been around for weeks. I grabbed an old backpack from under the bar, shoved the money into it and walked down to the bank with Jerry.

"He's such a loser," he griped. "Can't you get somebody better to handle the joint?"

"Nope. Anybody better would wanna make changes and start asking for medical insurance, a raise, and all manner of shit."

At the entrance to the Chase bank on Royal Street, I hesitated. I had a feeling Don hadn't made out any deposit slips.

"Holy crap," Jerry said, examining some of the checks Don had clipped together. "Some of these are a few months old. He lets people pay for drinks with checks?"

"Naw. Pool hall club membership."

"People pay to be members of that shit hole?"

"Yeah. Now help me endorse these checks, will ya?"

I wrote out the account number on a deposit slip and gave it to him. He started signing the backs of the checks with the account number, recording the check numbers on front. I signed off on each one and realized we had quite a haul here, including the cash and credit card receipts, which I held onto to check on later.

We took everything over to one of the tellers.

She raised a brow at me. "How come somebody torched your fabulous bakery but left that rat hole intact?"

"Good question," Jerry said.

I was pissed at them both. I felt a smug sense of satisfaction when I slid over a huge bag of pennies for her to count.

Taking care of all of this left us with about ten minutes to meet my sister. She was in a rotten mood by the time we turned up at the hole that used to be her bakery over on Decatur.

She and Judd were there, minus the kids.

"Where are they?" I asked as Sue Ellen and Cherise rolled up in the scariest bouffant hairdos this side of the 1960s. June thought they looked great. I was worried about either woman getting a helmet over their new do. It just wouldn't happen.

"Where are the kids?" I asked my sister again.

"With Judd's mom," she snapped. "Have you made contact with the people next door?"

"I just got here." It shocked me that she'd entrusted the kids with Judd's mom, a sweet but weirdo voodoo priestess who had a shop front business selling tarot readings, hot tea, and what she called Hoodoo Magic, over near Congo Square. Judd and June went through long periods of not speaking to her. I guessed in an emergency, she was worth talking to.

My cell phone rang. My heart did the Macarena in my chest when I saw Diego's name on the screen.

"Gotta take this," I muttered and moved away.

"You okay?" he asked. His voice filled me with the kind of equilibrium I didn't experience much in life. I wished he was here. I wanted to hold him. Not fuck him. Well, that, too. But I would have done anything for five minutes in his arms.

"My mom called and told me what happened," he said. "Are you all right?"

"Not really."

A long pause. "Call me when you're done. I'll come meet you." And with that, he ended the call, leaving me feeling buoyant and ready for anything.

I walked around the burned-out store. The insurance company guy was there, apparently on his second visit. He had asked her to fill out paperwork, and he'd also requested proof of recent upgrades to the business.

I'd given June Gold the money to open the place initially, and I'd also paid for two extensive remodels, facts she seemed to have forgotten. She had kept the paperwork for every bit of work done to the bakery at my insistence, and the agent could see she'd invested heavily in upgrades. Her bakery had been an institution.

He promised her a check for five times what it had cost me to purchase the building and the land. "You'll have it in seven to ten business days," he said.

That was mighty quick for N'Orleans.

June turned to me. "Now go talk to whats-her-name's family. I want to buy that shop next door, Colby."

I saw the startled look on the insurance agent's face. "She's bossy," he mumbled as I walked over to the shop next door. It was closed, and a sign on the door indicated the family was grieving. There was an emergency number, and I called it, leaving a voicemail message.

June wasn't pleased that I hadn't made progress and turned her back on me.

"We're not going to ride with you," Sue Ellen told me and Jerry. "Judd's gonna drive me and Cherise, 'cause he's got some stuff to pick up back at the house." She patted her hairdo. "Can't spoil the do."

"No," I said. "You can't." Frankly, I was not upset. This would give me the chance to spend some time with Diego.

My sister walked off in a huff as her husband drove off with the older women.

"Geez, I'm glad I'm gay," Jerry said, putting his arm around my shoulder. "Women are so fucking complicated."

I grinned. *And men weren't?*

"Hey," he said, looking embarrassed. "I got me a date."

"Oh, God. Who with?"

"Calvin," he whispered.

I stared at him. "For real this time?" I didn't feel good about him fooling around with my dad's boyfriend, but my dad didn't seem to mind. "Did you talk to him in person, Jerry?"

He rolled his eyes at me. "Of course. I'm not gonna let myself get ambushed again." He must have realized how apprehensive I was. "I'm smarter now. Whatever hold Teresa had on my brains and balls is gone."

"Well, that's something."

We gave each other a hug and Jerry said, "Why are you giving her more money? She treats you like shit."

I shrugged. "I want access to the kids."

He blew out a sigh. "I shoulda guessed. You're too good for this world sometimes, buddy." He gave me another hug, mounted his chopper, and left me standing there with the air out of my soul's tires.

I called Diego and wasn't surprised to get his voicemail. I left the chopper where it was and walked. I had no plan, really, but wanted to chew over things in my mind. I must have walked about an hour or so, my feet hurting, when Diego called me back.

"Sorry I got delayed. I've been organizing the funerals for Dave, Jackson, and Giles." He paused. "I'm in New Orleans.

Just stopped in to see Dave's mom. She had no idea he was even in a biker gang."

"How'd he keep that a secret?"

"Just sneaky, I guess. Now, where are you?"

"Near Magazine Street."

"Cool. I'm not far. There's a great hole-in-the-wall bar there."

"Yeah," I responded, "Ms. Mae's."

"That's the one. Meet you there in fifteen minutes." Once again, he ended our call, and I headed down the street. I came upon a mobile pet adoption unit. Usually, my normal reaction is to avert my gaze. I love animals but was never allowed to have them as kid. As an adult, I'd had a wonderful German Shepherd called Freddie, and I lost him to cancer. It had been three years, but the pain still gripped me.

I didn't want to look. I shouldn't have looked, but I did.

God. All those abandoned angels. They lay on ripped blankets and sheets, one to a cage or gated enclosure. I walked past each one, ignoring the imploring looks. What the hell was I doing? I had no space in my life for a dog.

I turned around and was ready to leave when I saw her.

Her face turned to me, and my heart broke. She was a small blue-nosed pit bull with the bluest eyes I'd ever seen. What tore at me was that one ear and half of the top of her mouth was missing.

I could hear Eva Cassidy's voice in my heart.

"What's her name?" I asked the young woman sitting beside her. I asked her that before I asked her anything about her injuries.

I knew before she told me—just knew what she was going to say.

"Her name is Beauty," she said in a tone that seemed defensive.

"Beauty," I said and dropped down to the ground. I

wanted to touch her. I had to touch her. I put my fingers through the small squares of Beauty's gated enclosure, and she gave them a tentative sniff.

"Can I hold her?"

The woman looking after her seemed shocked. "Of course." She leashed the dog and let her out, holding on to the leash as I sat cross-legged on the ground. Beauty climbed into my lap like she'd lived there all her life.

I knew then.

Garnet Beauty was gone.

She was gone.

And now I had another angel baby to love. Garnet had sent the most needy one she knew—one that needed all my love and would give hers to me.

Beauty looked up at me from blue eyes that had seen too much misery and known too much pain.

I couldn't stop the tears then, and she reached up and licked the tears from my chin. I held her. I wouldn't let her fall. I wouldn't let anyone hurt her ever again.

"She was a bait dog, and we found her six weeks ago tied to a fence and left to die," the woman told me. "We have no idea how she survived. She should be dead."

*I won't let you fall. I won't let you die.* I said these words silently, rocking back and forth with Beauty in my arms. She licked whatever part of my skin she could reach. I stopped crying. I needed to be strong.

"How long has it been?" the woman asked.

I looked at her, swiping at my eyes with the back of my hands.

"How long has it been since you lost your dog?" she clarified, her tone gentle and warm.

"Three years." I began to panic that maybe somebody else wanted Beauty. "Is she available?" Beauty felt thin to me.

"She's available." The woman smiled.

"Hello," a voice beside us said. I looked up, and my heart filled with hope when I saw Diego. He took it all in, me, the dog, everything. He knew it all.

"And who's this?" he asked, his voice tender.

"Beauty," I told him, my tone defensive now.

"Perfect name." He stroked the dog's head and chin. She gave him a lick.

"We have to do a home check," the woman said.

God. I hadn't thought about that.

"Colby's staying with my mom," Diego said. "Beauty will have a big house and people who love her. How soon can you come and check it out?"

I let him negotiate. The woman asked if I wanted to view Beauty's records. She seemed so happy that somebody wanted this precious dog. Of course I wanted her. I didn't want to let her go.

"I'm going to buy her for you," Diego said. He glanced at the woman. "We're willing to pay for any medical care she needs."

The woman talked about a replacement top lip being a possibility. Beauty had some health issues but nothing fatal.

I held my new girl tighter, and she sighed in my arms, falling asleep.

"How weird," the woman whispered. "She's notorious for never going to sleep."

"It's him," Diego said, jerking his thumb to me. "Beauty knows a good guy when she sees one."

I didn't want to say goodbye to her, but until the following afternoon, I had to. I held her and held her, knowing she was safe, knowing she would soon come to live with me. She whined as Diego walked away. We'd been there so long, darkness had started to settle. I'd had no idea.

He briefly touched my hand as we walked. I gazed up at the seductive moon and realized I was getting a fresh start.

A whole new life.

"Let me buy you a drink," I told Diego, who suddenly kissed me.

We grinned at each other. Obviously, the moon had cast its spell on him, too. We walked on down to the bar, and I wondered how long it would be before I could lay my lips and hands on him again.

Excerpt

The day of the funeral for Dave, Jackson, and Giles was a long day. And of course, the guys wanted to party in their names back at the club later. I just wanted to crawl into a hole somewhere and sleep. It wasn't so much the funeral that had been exhausting, it was everything around it. I'd talked at length to Badger, leader of the Texas Crushers, and I was now convinced they'd had nothing to do with the attack on the clubhouse.

Since Badger had made an overture to me before I'd taken Chase's place as leader, it would have been counterproductive to attack us now.

Cledus, Colby's father, despised the Texas Crushers. He just kept shooting his mouth off about how we should be organizing an attack on 'the bastards.' Frankly, I was tired of hearing it.

Chase had made an appearance in the procession but had disappeared before we all went back to the clubhouse. He didn't seem ready yet to come back to the club. He was still licking his wounds. I didn't blame him. The man had his pride.

Aside from Cledus trying to rile up everyone about the TC, I was being pressured to pick a vice president and an enforcer. That was a problem. The enforcer's job was to protect the president's ass. There was no one better qualified for the job than me. So, guess I'd have to rely on the entire club for that. As for vice president, I would have loved to appoint Colby, but I knew that was impossible. It would look suspicious and not make a shred of sense to any of the others given that he hadn't been with us very long.

Colby had come to the Banni from a smaller club called Death Proof, who got on the wrong side of the TC. Due to some lucrative drug business, the TC tried to get rid of Death Proof. Colby and a few others were taken into Banni protection and were now full-fledged members. The fact that Colby and I had secretively been lovers was neither here nor there, and, in fact, I was desperately trying to wean myself off Colby's lovin'.

It had been days since I'd pulled Colby into the woods and fucked him. He'd already told me he loved me. And yes, I loved him, too, but I couldn't say it. I wouldn't. Loving another man wasn't something the Banni would tolerate.

I'd been recruited to this club by the man I'd put down in the dirt a few days before. I'd had no choice but to take his place, although deep down I guess I knew it was my destiny all along. A promising career in the NFL was out of the question once my knees got screwed up in an underground fight. That recruiter never got to see me play. I'd had to do the fight so my mother wouldn't lose her house. After that, it was just fight after fight and lots of drugs to kill the pain.

When the leader of the Banni saved me from drug dealers I owed a fortune to, I became their enforcer. I was the one the club sent when they wanted to make someone's blood run cold when they wanted to send a clear message. There were times when I just turned off my feelings altogether.

Now, the only time I felt vulnerable, the only time I felt as if someone could crush me with a single word, was when I was in Colby's arms.

It was the most wonderful yet the scariest place in the world for me. I was as addicted to Colby as I had been to painkillers. Didn't matter that either one of them could bring my life to an abrupt end. I'd finished with the drugs a long time ago, and I never thought I'd find anything harder to quit than that. But I'd been wrong. My addiction to Colby was ten times stronger than drugs.

I looked around now at the men and women in this room. They were all drunk and sad, hoisting their glasses up to the three large photographs of their fallen comrades that some of the women had hung up on the wall for the occasion. Three wasted lives, but then they'd been pretty well wasted before they'd died, as was my own.

I glanced over to see Colby sitting with Jerry and Marcel, his dog, Beauty, curled up at his feet. Pure love between those two, man and beast, not to mention the entire club who'd kinda made Beauty their mascot. Beauty was a friendly dog, trusting, and Beauty loved anyone and everyone who'd love her and feed her treats. It was nice having the dog around.

Nuts came over and sat beside me now. He placed a hand on my shoulder. "What are you doing over here by yourself?"

"Thinking," I told him.

"You going to keep me VP or what?" He passed me some nuts. The guy had earned his nickname that way.

I took a few cashews and tossed them into my mouth. "You want to be my VP?"

"Yeah," he said. "But it's your call, Boss."

"I'll take care of it tomorrow at church. Right now, I'm beat."

He nodded, standing up. "Why don't you take Tammy with you and lay down in the back?" Nuts glanced over to where Tammy sat with two of the other biker chicks. "When you going to make her legit?"

I met his gaze. "Is it a problem I want to be on my own?"

"No. But there are questions about why you don't take on an ol' lady. Only natural you have someone. Everyone does."

Great. Fucking great. "You spreading shit about me now, Nuts?" I asked, trying to hold onto my temper.

"No, man." He shook his head. "Just Tammy's been wanting to know. She wonders why you don't give it to her more often. She's been saying it's been months. You got someone else, that's cool. I know you must be getting laid somewhere, man."

Before Colby, I went out for sex, off somewhere, without the colors on my back, fucking all kinds of strangers. Tammy was my cover. I fucked her once in a while to keep the speculation about my sexuality away. Girls hung out, danced, got naked, got fucked by the guys in the club all the time. I usually tried to avoid those gangbangs. Sometimes I had no choice but to participate. It wasn't easy to get hard. Girls didn't do it for me, never had. It was just the way I was made. I'd have to focus on one of the guys and imagine I was doing him.

Poor Tammy had gotten a raw deal from me. I knew from the look on Nuts' face that the time had come for me to take her to bed again. If I didn't, there was going to be talk, some innuendos. I couldn't have that.

"It's a good idea," I told him. I needed to talk to Tammy anyway, to get her to stop complaining about the lack of attention she was getting from me. I got up and walked over to where Tammy was sitting with the girls. I knew some of the guys were watching, one of them being Colby.

Tammy looked up at me and smiled. Jesus, I hated playing the role of some Neanderthal caveman, but I was the leader now. I had to give them a show, shut them up for a while. "Hey, baby," she said.

I reached out for her and pulled her out of the chair and up into my arms. I placed my hands on her ass, dragged her close and kissed her like there was no tomorrow. I heard the guys all catcall and cheer. Tammy put her hands in my hair. She was enjoying the kiss. I felt absolutely nothing.

The cheers and wolf whistles grew louder. I grinned at my audience, scooped Tammy up and flung her over my shoulder. I carried her off down the hallway, trying hard not to think about Colby and how he was feeling. If I'd been him, it wouldn't have been great.

I could do this. I could make love to Tammy by imagining Colby lying there in that bed. That would get me hard. And since Tammy expected hard and fast from me, that's what I gave her. There was a part of me I'd only ever shown Colby in bed, a tender, vulnerable, loving side.

Tammy fell asleep in my arms. I lay there with my eyes wide open, thinking about how I couldn't risk anyone questioning my sexuality. In spite of that fact, I felt truly ashamed. I hadn't hurt Tammy in any physical way. I'd given her exactly what she wanted, and I'd made sure she got off. I stayed hard the entire time, so it was good for her. It sucked for me. It was the price I had to pay.

Could I do this over and over? If I had to, I guess I could, but I knew I'd be putting it off, making excuses. Everyone, including this girl, was waiting for me to make it official, to declare Tammy my ol' lady but I didn't want anyone on the back of my bike, or in my bed, except Colby. It just wasn't going to be.

# ABOUT THE AUTHORS

A.J. Llewellyn is the author of almost three hundred published gay romance novels. A.J. lives in California, but dreams of living in Hawaii. Frequent trips to all the islands, bags of Kona coffee in the fridge and a healthy collection of Hawaiian records keep A.J. refueled.

A.J's passion for the islands led to writing a play about the last ruling monarch of Hawaii, Queen Lili'uokalani. A.J. has written a non-erotic novel about the overthrow of her kingdom written in diary form from her maid's point of view.

A.J. never lacks inspiration for male/male erotic romances and has to prise fingers from the computer keyboard to pursue other passions: collecting books on Hawaiiana, surfing and spending time with family, friends and animal companions.

D.J. Manly: I write not only for my own pleasure but for the pleasure of my readers. I can't remember a time in my life when I haven't written and told stories. When I'm not writing, I'm dreaming about writing, doing something wild and adventurous, or trying to make the world a better and more open-minded place to live in. I adore beautiful men, and I know I'm not alone in this! Eroticism between consenting adults, in all its many forms, is the icing on the cake of life!

D.J. has published well over two-hundred novels/novellas and is a well-seasoned writer.

www.ingramcontent.com/pod-product-compliance
Lightning Source LLC
Chambersburg PA
CBHW060831120626
46557CB00001B/460